Lock Down Publications and Ca$h
Presents

I0637414

TIPPIN THE SCALES 3

Play No Games

Written By
Christopher "Diesel" Hornezes

First Edition 2025

Printed in the United States of America

This is a work of fiction. Names, characters, places, and incidents either are products of the author's imagination or are used fictitiously. Any similarity to actual events or locales or persons, living or dead, is entirely coincidental.

Lock Down Publications
P.O. Box 944
Stockbridge, GA 30281
www.lockdownpublications.com

Like our page on Facebook: Lock Down Publications
www.facebook.com/lockdownpublications.ldp

Stay Connected with Us!

Text **LOCKDOWN** to 22828 to stay up-to-date with new releases, sneak peaks, contests and more…

Like our page on Facebook:
Lock Down Publications

Join Lock Down Publications/The New Era Reading Group

Visit our website:
www.lockdownpublications.com

Follow us on Instagram:
Lock Down Publications

Email Us: We want to hear from you!

Acknowledgements

Yo, everyone says this, but real rap, God is good! Even when you turn away from Him because it seems like He left your side, He is still there. I say this to all of y'all who doubt that. Trust and believe. I swear to you that He is in your corner like people only claim to be.

I got to shout out to you, Ca$h! You been real good to me, man. It took some hard work to get you to see my potential, and now that you do, the sky is *not* the limit.

To my brothers, CJ, DRE, my homies, Youngblood, Memphis, TROUBLESOME, and to all the guys: AMOR! To all of y'all buying my books, supporting me, mad love to all of y'all, yo. On my dead homies, I love y'all.

To every hater that spoke ill of me but was too bitch made to come holla at me in the cell, love y'all bitch ass niggaz too. Y'all the ones that really motivated me. Get mad. IDGAF.

Shorty, Duwap, Queen Naija, Crazy Red, P Real, G Ball, Biker Girl, Guera, Spirit, Foxy Mama! WHAZ HANIN!

To all of my LDP family! LOVE, YO!

And lastly, to my close friend, Mattie, yo, Ma, you and I are crazy, but no matter the bumps we hit, our path always levels out. That doesn't happen for everyone. I love you, Ma. Real rap. God bless you and your family and those talented young ladies you're turning into potential stars.

Chapter 1

Brrrrrrrr! Brrrrrrrr! Brrrrrrrr! Brrrrrrrr! Brrrrrrrr!
Carmelo squeezed the triggers on both of his Uzis then ran back to Rodrigo's SS Trailblazer, jumping in the front. Rodrigo hit the gas and took off, leaving the Escalade at the light.

"Yeah! Yeah! Half a million, baaybeeee!" Carmelo shouted, geeked as hell to have just done what so many others had failed to do.

"Aye, Melo?" Rodrigo hollered over to him over the loud roar of the supercharged V8 engine under the SUV's hood.

Carmelo, still gripping the twin spitters, was looking in the mirror. He could still see the Escalade at the light, not moving. He grew so excited that he wanted to post what he had done on social media to brag about it.

"Melo!"

"What, nigga?!" Carmelo snapped, not liking his homie taking him out of his thoughts of what he was going to do with his share of the money that had been put on the young, rich, Dominican's head.

He turned to his left and found himself looking into the barrel of Rodrigo's Mac 11. He opened his mouth to shout, but Rodrigo squeezed the trigger before he could get a word out. Bullets ripped through Carmelo's face, exploding out the back of his head. His brains flew out the window, landing on the side of the highway as Rodrigo sped down 41.

"That would be my half million, my nigga. Good lookin' out for the help though, king," he said then reached over to open the passenger's door and pushed the dead man out.

He pulled the door closed and slowed down a little, knowing another weight station was ahead but not knowing if it was opened or closed. He reached to grab his phone from the center console and called his big homie back to report the mission a success.

"Yo' ass better have some good news for me, king."

"Hell yeah, I do, brotha! I got him! And Melo gon' too, joe!"

Rodrigo heard the man chuckle.

"I knew you was a real ass nigga when I brought you home. Cool. I got that chicken for you when you get back up to the Mil, aight?"

Right as Rodrigo was about to speak, his rear window exploded, startling him so much that he shrieked and swerved, nearly crashing into the center concrete highway divider.

"What the fuck?!" he said to himself, looking in the rearview mirror.

"What was that, nigga?" his big homie asked.

Rodrigo's jaw dropped when he saw the Escalade on his ass just a few hundred feet away.

"King! What the fuck was that sound, nigga?"

"Aye! I'ma hit'chu back, joe!" Rodrigo shouted then ended the call and tossed his phone. "Fuck!" he then cursed as bullets flew into his SUV, shattering his windshield from within.

***

JAVI

He had the Escalade's gas pedal to the floor. The insanely powerful, supercharged, and intercooled engine under the hood roared out of the twin Borla exhaust pipes. His speedometer read that he was pushing more than one hundred twenty miles an hour. The black Chevy Trailblazer SS was in his sights, half a mile up ahead of him. He was gaining on it... fast.

"Guess they think I ride in whips that ain't bulletproof," Javi chuckled. "You ready, bae?" Javi asked his woman, gripping his steering wheel with one hand.

Riding next to him, with their two big, black and brown, tiger-striped cane corsos on the back of the Ext, Michelle had a fully-automatic Heckler & Koch G36, fitted with a one hundred-round drum, in her hands, gripping it tightly.

"I was ready the second them bitch ass niggas interrupted me, yo!" she spat angrily in her New York accent.

Before the man had appeared at Javi's window while they were waiting at a red light, Michelle was giving her man some toe-curling oral, making his eyes roll to the back of his head. They had been enroute from Javi's yard to grab a bite to eat after a hell of a night where they both nearly lost their lives when two semi-trucks driven by two men, who worked for Victor Gomez, prince of the Rojas-Gomez Cartel, and shooters from an overpass near Caledonia, Wisconsin attempted to take Javi and his woman out. They were unsuccessful, as so many had been before, but they had come really close... way too close.

The beef between Javi and Victor was ongoing, but in the recent weeks, bodies had begun to drop every day, and bloodshed was all over Wauk-Town, painting the town red. Javi focused his eyes on the rear of the SUV. Getting closer, Michelle reached up and hit the button to open the sunroof. Javi reached for her and held onto her as she stood up through it with her gun. She took aim at the rear window and squeezed the trigger, blowing it out. The driver swerved hard, damn near hitting the center divider. She kept dumping at it, sending round after round through the blown out rear window, aiming at the driver as they blew through the intersection for 41 and Wadsworth Road.

"Shit, shit, shit, shit!" Rodrigo panicked as bullets continuously flew into his SS, coming so close to hitting him that he couldn't even put his head up, or it would get blown off of his shoulders.

The dash blew out as slugs slammed into it. Sparks flew out and blinded Rodrigo. He let go of the wheel as the fiery hot sparks flew into his eyes. He screamed in pain. Then, an explosion from under his Trailblazer made the entire SUV shoot up off the ground, going airborne. Rodrigo screamed in fear as he realized that he was in the air, flying over the center divider, and entering the on-coming traffic side of the highway. Seconds later, he landed right in the middle of the northbound traffic lanes, right in the path of a fuel tanker on a late-night run to deliver gas to the gas station that they had just passed at the intersection.

Booom!

"Wooooo! Hahahaaa, muthafuckaaaa!" Javi shouted as the driver of the tanker brazenly jumped out of his rig seconds before it collided with the Trailblazer and exploded in a massive fireball.

"Pendejo," Michelle muttered, sinking back down into the Escalade then closing the sunroof.

"Cono, Michelle! Have I told you how much I love you today?" he asked, entering the underside of Gurnee.

"I do not believe you have. Asi que, let's hear it, nigga," Michelle said, smiling all cheesy at him.

He laughed his ass off again then let the words of thug love flow from his lips. Michelle scooted to him and got her a kiss then grabbed his iPhone to make a call.

"Dimelo, lil cutty," answered Javi's big cousin, Danny, head honcho of the cocaine-rich Valdez family.

Javi enlightened Danny on what had just taken place. Coming to the intersection of 41 and Stern School Road, Javi bent a right turn and got up off of the highway, hurrying to get to his woman's home to put the Caddy truck up.

"Okay. Aight. These bitch ass niggas is getting out they bodies right now, yo! Homies!" Danny exploded. "Where are y'all at now?"

"Headin' to the crib, but I got some biz to handle for Sol, so we gone switch the whip and shoot back to the yard."

"And get some food!" Michelle reminded him, still starving.

"Yeah, and get some food," he told Danny.

"Handle it. ChaCha gon' hit chu up in a minute, yo. Y'all be cool."

"Yup. Love, cuz."

"Bye, Danny!" Michelle hollered out then.

"One," Danny said to them both then ended the call.

"Big cuz gon' declare nuclear war on them bitches, bae," Javi chuckled, knowing exactly how his older cousin got down and the connection he had to make it happen, but more than that… Danny had ChaCha.

Javier Valdez, born and raised in Waukegan, Illinois, a.k.a. Waulk-Town, was the product of Dominican royalty. His father and mother were certified killers, fearless when it came to gun play, and geniuses when it came to bringing in the family's famous white-gold from the Dominican Republic, no middle man.

Javier was the owner of a multi-million dollar trucking company and rolling with him was a crew of loyal riders that had all come up out the mud. Also with Javi was his younger brother, Xavier, and their baby sister, Evelyn. The three of them had followed the footsteps of their mother, their father, and their parents' cousins, who they themselves had entered the unbelievably intricate world of drugs importing and trafficking via the original three Valdez brothers – the deceased Pedro, who was the oldest, Juanito, the middle child and grease monkey, and the youngest and rowdiest of the three, Javi and his siblings' grandfather, Diego.

Javi, Xavier, and Evelyn were led to cocaine-god riches by the matriarch of the family, ChaCha, who was the right hand of the head honcho. The two together, to Javi, his brother, and sister were like big bro/ big sis, big cuz, and Ma and Pops, guiding the youngest of the family. Even while incarcerated, Danny ruled with a mighty fist, keeping his family's name and business intact, while ChaCha enforced his laws on the streets with zero tolerance for bullshit. They were a big, happy, ridiculously rich family. Anyone that opposed them... died... painfully.

"Weeell..." Michelle said, ready to finish what she was doing when the clown foolishly ran up on Javi's bulletproof Escalade. "Now that that is over with."

A mischievous smile grew on her face as she reached behind her where she and Javi's two big, muscular, black and brown, brindle cane corsos, Demon and Diamond, sat restlessly after the chaos to put the G36 back into the hidden gun rack under the rear passenger's seat.

"Where were we?"

She then reached over to undo Javi's pants again and got back to pleasing him. The second she freed his length again, her head was back in his lap, and all nine of his inches were in her mouth.

***

EVELYN

"Hello?"

"Whaz' hanin', lil mama? This Prince, the guy you met at the gas station earlier."

Evelyn gasped. "Oh, wow! Hey! Um... damn, how you get my number cause I sho forgot to give it to you before my b... my friend started acting crazy."

"I saw the number on the side of your truck; I took a guess that it was yours, and sure enough, a nigga was right!"

Evelyn couldn't help but laugh at how geeked he sounded. She was actually glad to hear from him.

The twenty-one-year-old was the youngest in the Valdez family. She was the wild child with Rosa Acosta beauty. As the boss of her big brother's company's auto-transportation division, Evelyn ran the show with six other lady truckers that drove for her. When Evelyn wasn't behind the wheel of her big Volvo 780, she was with her long-time girlfriend, Gloria, kicking up some sort of drama somewhere, somehow.

"Resourceful, aren't we?" she replied with a chuckle.

"I mean, I wasn't tryna be creepy 'n shit, but when a nigga like me meets a woman like you, on God, I got to see what's to it."

"A woman like me?" Evelyn asked, as she cruised along the highway at the speed limit in her long and tall, car-carrier, semi-truck with her girlfriend and two of the drivers, Payton and Olivia, trailing behind with a motorcade of armed Jamaicans bringing up the rear, watching over the ladies. "What exactly does that mean, Prince, if I may ask? Does it mean showstopper?"

"No."

Evelyn's face fell in her lap then.

But then Prince added, "You are the show, and I would bet everything that can't nobody stop you."

Evelyn's smile immediately returned. She suddenly found herself wishing that the tall, dark, and handsome man was there with her, so she could see that smile that had nearly made her forget that she was a lesbian and had a girlfriend.

"Anyways, though," Prince continued, "what's the chances of you lettin' me take you out sometime? I cannot make myself think of anything other than you and that beautiful smile, Eve. And you have a pig."

Evelyn burst out laughing. Glancing over to her right, she reached down and picked up her brown, furry, mini, baby potbelly piglet lying by the shifter to her thirteen-speed transmission.

"His name is Oinky, but sometimes, we call him the Notorious P.I.G.," Evelyn joked.

"That's wild, but it's different," he replied, laughing at her.

"So, how is your day goin' today, Prince?" she asked with her left hand steering her truck, right hand giving Oinky a belly rub.

"Crazy. My dumb ass cousin is the definition of the word idiot. How you say that in Spanish?"

"Idiota. Peudejo."

"Yeah. His ass is all of that."

"What did he do, if you don't mind me askin'?"

"Tryna be too gangsta for his own good; he a hot ass firecracker soaked in jet fuel. He runnin' from twelve and a bunch of people he pissed off."

"Wow. Well, I guess he gots to learn a lesson, huh?"

"Yep. Me havin' to come out to Waukegan and post up with him because his ass is scared to death, that's fuckin' with my business."

"Family can be what one needs to get it together," Evelyn preached, knowing that her family never let anyone fall without being there to help them right back up,

"But family can also be each other's downfall," Prince countered, knowing all too well how families had members that were so dysfunctional that when someone tried to help them, they got their own worlds shattered.

"Honestly though, Eve, I don't wanna talk about him; I wanna talk about when you gon' let a nigga take you out? Dinner? A movie? A walk on the beach?"

"A walk on the beach though?" Evelyn chuckled.

"You don't like that stuff?"

"I mean… I'm a Dominican woman; I am all about sandy beaches and clear water, but it's just… picturin' you walkin' on a beach, holdin' hands wit' a chick, is funny."

Prince laughed. "I might be from the hood, but I'm not yo' average dude, Eve. When I have a woman in my life that I actually want, I show it. Fuck talkin' about it; I'm 'bout action."

Evelyn's smile gave her chipmunk cheeks. The man was killing her softly with his song, and she was loving it.

"Tell me anything, Prince," she told him, wanting to hear what he had to say about that.

"Why would I do that? The only thing that's relevant is you lettin' me take you out for a fun-filled evenin.'"

Dammit, man! This nigga here! she thought to herself, thinking he would have said something corny, so she could find a reason to resist him.

"I'll think about it," Evelyn said instead.

"That's all I ask. When you ready for a real man to make you smile and to make you happy, make sure you call me, Eve. I'll put you first."

"We'll see," she told him, then she ended the call while she was still in human form instead of a puddle in her seat.

Chapter 2

"Hey, ladies? What seems to be the problem?" asked Ignacio, owner of the Mexican restaurant, when one of his waiters brought him to a table with three gorgeous women that had some complaints.

"Well, for starters," sassed the chick with deep brown skin that was like pancake syrup, exotic, Asian like, slanted eyes, and a femininely raspy voice, "the food here sucks!"

"And secondly," came the high-yellow complexion woman, sitting next to the chink eyed girl, "your boss decided it was okay to kick some shit up, so we gon' return the favor."

Ignacio's eyebrows rose as he got nervous. He took a step back, glancing from side to side. None of his customers were paying any attention to him or the scowling ladies.

"I… I'm… not sure what you're talking about. I own this restaurant; I don't have a boss."

"Sure, you do," said the third chick, a creamy caramel beauty that was so gorgeous that the evil etched into her face still made Ignacio unable to stop staring at her.

"You don't own this restaurant. Victor Gomez does; you just launder his money for him," she said, then with the blink of an eye, she jumped up from her seat with a machete in her hand. "And now you die for him!" she added with a sinister grin.

Ignacio then heard screaming and shouting, followed by the shattering glass. He looked and saw his customers fleeing from the blown-out wall of windows that lined the front of his restaurant. A mob of masked goons with assault rifles had run in and started dumping, targeting what seemed to be only his staff members. Ignacio turned back to the girl to see that she had wound up for the head-chop swing.

"Wait!" he screamed out.

Boom!

Right before she could swing the machete and behead him, a loud blast came. His head exploded into chunks, putting a damper in her plans. Her jaw dropped when his body hit the floor. To the right of him, she saw the big, tall, muscular, blue-gray eyed man that had been hers for years gripping his big .45 Desert Eagle in his hand, grinning at her.

"You fucking asshole! That was my kill, dammit!" she snapped.

***

MACHO

Macho burst out laughing as his brother, City Cee, and also Dee and Lacey blew down the restaurant's staff members with no mercy while allowing those that were not affiliates of Victor Gomez, or employees of his affiliates, to run.

"Oooooo, ya almost had it! Ya got to be quicker than that!" Macho laughed, teasing his Nuyorican goddess, Yessinia.

G-Baby, standing by Yessy's side, caught sight of who she and Yessy knew was the Rojas-Gomez Cartel's money laundering supervisor, based off the pictures they had been shown by ChaCha, trying to make a break for it. She took off running after him. Felicia followed like the ride or die chick that she was. G-Baby jumped up and dunked herself on him, taking him to the ground. Felicia grabbed one side of him while G-Baby held the other. Yessy ran over as he screamed and pleaded for mercy.

"Shut up, bitch!" Yessy shouted, then she swung the machete as hard as she could and cut right through the center of his face.

The top of his head flew off somewhere. G-Baby and Felicia let his body drop to the floor. Blood immediately began spewing out and pooling around him. Yessy turned and looked at her man with a scowl on her face.

"If you take any more of my kills, I'ma beat your ass, yo."

"Then be faster, punk," Macho said with a smirk.

Yessy nodded. "Bet. On the next one, mamao," she called him. "Ladies, let's go! It's on now!"

Without a word more, the three women ran up out of the restaurant, leaving Macho and his Steel City Mafia family inside. He watched his woman jump up behind the wheel of one of the big lifted-up Ford Excursions where her big German rottweiler and Macho's tiger-brindle red nose pitbull awaited. G-Baby hopped up into the passenger's seat and Felicia in the rear. Yessy mashed the gas and peeled off in a rush to get to the next Rojas-Gomez owned business to get her kills up.

Macho shook his head then called his people. The seven of them left the bloody restaurant and hopped up into the other Excursion. Behind the wheel, Tool dipped up out of the lot before the first cop car could show up. He sped off to get to their next hit spot with murder on his mind for the attempt made on the lives of his little cousin, Javi, and his woman.

***

JAVI

"Wow…" Javi ended the call and started laughing his ass off as he cruised east, heading down Wadsworth Road, enroute to the Beach Park area of north eastern Illinois where his and his woman's tucked away log cabin style mansion was.

Michelle looked over at him.

"What happened?"

"Bae, cuzzo 'n 'nem are still out there kickin' shit off!" he told her. "They just blew down 'erybody in that one crappy ass Mexican restaurant over in Waulk-Town, the one with them punk ass $1 steak tacos."

Michelle burst out laughing then.

"Fuck it. The food there sucked anyways, yo. Good riddance to them sour ass tacos."

"Straight up. The Steel City Mafia don't play no games when it comes to murderin' people," Javi said, unable to think of a single time that his cousins and their self-made gang hadn't gone over hard to eliminate all that opposed them and then laughed like maniacs, competing for kills like they were engrossed in a live game of *Call of Duty: Black Ops* zombie missions.

Passing a line of tall, thick trees that hid all that was behind them, Javi reached the entrance to his stone paved driveway and turned in. He rolled along the curved and inclining driveway with a deep and long running creek on the left and a tall stone retaining wall to the right. A minute later, he pulled up to the grand mansion that he and his woman dreamed up and had built to perfection with a matching ten-car garage to go with it.

Javi parked his Escalade at the garage next to his brand-new McLaren P1 that he had just gotten for his twenty-fifth birthday and killed the engine. He opened his door and hopped out, going around to help his woman down from the thirty inches up in the air from the big Forgiato rims the extended Caddy pickup truck rolled on.

"Don't think we comin' up outta here before we settle that hot shit you was poppin' at the yard," Michelle said as he let the dogs out the backseat.

"You talkin' like I forgot all that shit yo' ass was talkin'," Javi chuckled. "Let's go handle that, then we gon' go get this money, baby."

Michelle smirked at him mischievously with some very freaky thoughts in her head.

"¡Chacho, *mami*! ¡Mira la patras!" Javi exclaimed and smacked her plump ass hard. "That ass is phat!"

She burst out laughing at him.

"Booty fiend ass, nigga."

"Damn right, I love this phat, juicy culo," Javi stated proudly as he held her cheeks, walking her up to the door and squeezing then through her tight, leather, Givenchy pants while she entered the security code. "As soon as we get up in here, yo ass better let a nigga do what he does best, freca."

The door unlocked to a long, tall hall that led to the massive open concept first floor and the chef's style kitchen.

"And what might that be, Papi?" asked Michelle as Demon and Diamond ran into the house, excited to be home.

"Beatin' that wet ass pussy up like I'm Roy Jones Jr." Javi scooped her up again and hip closed the door.

"I hear you talkin'. Yet we still here instead of up in the bedroom," Michelle said re-issuing the challenge.

"Say less," Javi replied then took off running to get her to the bedroom and remind her that he would always and forever be that nigga that walked instead of talked.

***

Down in St. Petersburg, Florida

"Hola, Señora Gomez ¿Como te sientes?"

Valencia, a woman well into her late seventies, looked up at the caramel-brown skinned woman. She was tall and had a headful of steel gray hair with a warm, welcoming smile. Valencia was out on the deck, getting some sun in the private section of the massive retirement community that she owned, when the woman garbed in bright white scrubs, white sneakers, and rubber examination gloves spoke.

"Who are you? How did you get here?" Valencia asked the woman with furrowed brows.

"I am your new caretaker, señora. Soy Marla," she said and walked up next to her, looking out over the deck at the view of the ocean.

"I do not know you. Why have I never seen you before?" asked Valencia.

"I've worked all over the place, ma'am. It's so big in this community that you've made feel like a paradise. You might not actually get the chance to meet all of your employees, but Maria can vouch for me."

Hearing the woman mention the name of her primary caretaker of nearly a decade put Valencia at ease.

"¿Pere, donde esta ella?" She asked where Maria was.

"Maria has willfully given up her position to me," the woman told her. "Now, how about we get you inside, so we can get you ready for the day? You've got a very long one ahead of you."

"No! I am not going with you! Leave me!" Valencia refused, crossing her arms over her chest and pouting.

The lady shrugged then.

"Guess we'll do this the hard way then."

Valencia saw her pull a syringe from the front pocket of her uniform shirt. She gasped and went wide-eyed.

She screamed, "No! No! ¡Ayudame! Oscar! Pepe!" She tried to get up from her chair and get away.

Slap!

¡Ay!" Valencia cried out from the sting of the woman's open hand going across her face, making her fall to the desk's floor.

"¡Puta! ¡Callate la maldita boca!" the woman then hissed, crouching down next to Valencia. "¡Tu puto nieto va a repentir jodiendo con mi nieto!"

Maritza jammed the syringe into the crook of Valencia's neck and injected her with the powerful sedative. In seconds, the old queen of the Rojas-Gomez Cartel was out of it, numb to reality. The grandmother of Javier, Xavier, and Evelyn Valdez stood back up. She looked down at the disoriented woman with malice in her eyes. Martiza was past tired of the attempts made on her grandson. Her old life as enforcer and hit woman for her family's multi-million-dollar cocaine empire had, amongst all things in her sixty plus years of life, taught her that nothing was more important than family and protecting those that she loved. Coming out of retirement to snatch up Victor Gomez's grandmother was just one of her plans to make the Rojas-Gomez Cartel fall. At the current moment, her other plans were taking place.

The door opened up just then. Two massive Dominican men stepped out with Maritza's ox-built husband, Diego, behind them.

"¿Que 'stas hacienda, mi amor? We need to be going," Diego said urgently.

Maritza turned to her husband. Without a word, she left off of the big deck, walking through the lavish home, past all of the employees that she and her people had laid out enroute to get to Valencia Gomez. Outside, a black Sprinter van awaited. Posted up next to it was Diego's older, middle brother, Juanito, and Juanito's wife, Carolina.

"¿Todo bien?" Carolina asked, seeing tears in her sister-in-law's eyes.

"I will be when those fuckers are dead!" Maritza said then went and got up into the luxurious Mercedes, ready to continue with the plans.

She had nothing else to say on the topic. Nobody did. It was a wrap. The Rojas-Gomez Cartel had royally fucked up and were about to learn not to fuck with the Valdez family.

***

JAVI

"¡Aaaayyy, Paapiii! Oohh, shit! Yes! Goddammit!" Michelle cried out as Javi hit it hard and fast from the back in their big bed in their expansive master bedroom.

"Fuuuck! ¡Meteme, Javi! ¡Meteme duro!"

Javi clenched his teeth and put his back into it. He hit the pussy hard like he was pissed off at it. He pounded her so fast that it sounded like clapping. Her phat, juicy booty cheeks bounced like they were full of Jello, visually enticing Javi to the max.

"Shit! This pussy so good! Dammit!" Javi growled, gripping her hips and jack-hammering her.

Trina's *I Got a Problem* featuring Plies bumped from the expensive German brand audio system. Javi hit it relentlessly from the back after being on top and drilling her from the side. Michelle rode his dick until she'd reached her fourth climax, then Javi got her ass-up-face-down, so he could crack from the back and watch her ass cheeks jiggle.

He wrapped her hair around his hand, letting go of her hips. He tore it up so good that Michelle saw stars. She screamed out in ecstasy, then seconds after, she came for the fifth time, soaking Javi's dick all over again. Javi pulled out of her pussy after her orgasm. He grabbed her sweaty ass cheek and opened her up, exposing Michelle's puckered up asshole. Michelle squealed in delight when she felt him lean in and lick around the rim of her booty hole.

"Ooooo, you so nasty!" she moaned, loving it though.

Javi laughed as he licked. He spit on her asshole, then lifting himself back upright, he grabbed his cock and put the tip of it into her anus. Michelle put her face down on the bed and reached back to hold her cheeks open. She hissed from the momentary pain she felt from his stretching her out, but in seconds, it turned into pleasure.

He slow stroked her ass as Rick Ross' *Hit You From The Back* started playing. Javi was gentle on her but gave it to her the way that she demanded. He felt her clenching up around him, which brought him closer to his nut. As he felt it coming, his muscles tightened up as did his balls. He shouted out he was about to bust. Michelle looked back at him. She loved seeing his face when he came. Javi loved seeing her face as he pleased her. Her fuck faces were extraordinary.

"F-F-F-Fuuuuuuck!" Javi let out a deep, guttural groan as his nut came.

He pulled his dick out and skeeted all in Michelle's ass crack, emptying himself completely. Michelle giggled. The feeling of his hot droplets in her ass made her feel so dirty and sexy at the same time. Rough, kinky, nasty, hot was how she liked it, and Javi aimed to please.

"Wooo! Chea!" Javi plopped down on the bed next to her. "¡Diablo, bebe!"

Michelle burst out laughing as she looked at him.

"I be drainin' you, Papi. Lemme find out you can't handle me no more."

"Sheeeeeeeeeeeiiit! You got me all the way fucked up, punk!" Javi smacked her ass cheek. "¡Yo soy el hombre! ¡Nunca olvidalo!"

Michelle chuckled. "I hear you, tigueraso," she told him. "Aye, you know I still got that job to do too. This one, since I'm injured, I could use my big, strong, fearless, future hubby at my side. Whatcha' say, Papi?"

"I am all the way down, amor. Cuzzo 'n Yessy might wanna ride along too."

"They are more than welcome to help us rid the world of scum, babe. The more the merrier."

"Think they'll bring the Gangsta Boo?"

"Do they ever go anywhere without her?" Michelle replied.

Javi laughed. "Good point. Um... bae, I cannot stop wonderin' if cuzzo and G..."

"No," Michelle cut him off quickly.

Javi raised an eyebrow. "You don't even know what I was gon' say."

"Nigga, yes, I do. Everyone wonders if Macho's fuckin' Gabi, but he isn't. Do you know what Yessy would do to any woman that touched him?"

"I do, but I can't see Yessy doing to G-Baby what she did to that weird ass bitch in the club when cuz threw her that bash on her twenty-first birthday," Javi said.

Michelle cringed at the memory. They all had witnessed the wild Bronx girl, after Yessy had caught the girl slipping in the parking lot and snatched her up, chop the girl's fingers off and make her eat them one by one.

"Yessima is nuts, yo; she will never share her man with any woman, but do you remember what Macho did to that clown ass nigga that smacked Yessy's ass at the club we was at on his twenty-second b-day?" Michelle asked.

"That crazy ass nigga broke a muthafuckin' beer bottle and stabbed dude in his face with it, then he tossed him up over the bar," Javi said and laughed at the memory.

"What is it with you and him throwin' people over counters and bars, Javi?" Michelle wanted to know, thinking back to when she had stepped up to defend Evelyn from predatory eyes fucking on her at a Burger King in Waukegan, then Javi, Macho, and Tool popped up on the two men being creeps and ended up sending it up inside the BK, resulting in Macho tossing one guy over the counter and Javi the other, who just happened to be Kenzie's baby daddy.

Javi laughed. "Our dads used to get it busin' like that when they was wild'n. We just keepin' the tradition alive, baby."

Michelle smiled her ass off. "Dios mio. I love you, Javier."

"I love you too. Now, let's get cleaned up and head out. We got some money to make, and I need my beautiful future wife with me."

"I'm with you 'til death do us part, baby," she told him, dead ass.

***

XAVIER

"Lil' mama out like a broke light bulb," he told Kenzie, joining her on the big, oversized, Italian leather couch in his wide-open living room.

At his house, out in Zion off of Loreli Drive and Route 173, Xavier and Kenzie had gone to lay low and relax.

Neveah had been still so scared from the dramatic events from earlier with her mother. Xavier surprised Kenzie when he sung her daughter to sleep with a soft lullaby. It had her so hot for him that she had to get up out of the room, or he would be the one being taken to bed.

"Thank you, Xavier," Kenzie said, sighing. "I really appreciate all that you've done for us."

He nodded. "Ain't shit. Just hope my life don't scare you too much."

Kenzie chuckled. "Naw, boo-boo. I might be from out here in 'Zompton, but I'm a thoroughbred. I'm used to the streets."

"Oh, yeah? Why do I feel like you love gangsta shit?" he asked, looking at the thick, beautiful woman, wishing he could stop from lusting after her and that big, phat, round, juicy ass she had in those tight, red leggings.

Kenzie smiled mischievously. Instead of answering him with her words, she decided that there was no longer a point in hiding what she was feeling, so she got up from her spot, stepped in front of him, then with a finger, she pushed him back so that his back was against the couch's backrest. She climbed onto his lap then, straddling him. As she wrapped her arms around his neck, her big breasts were just inches away from his face. She gazed down into Xavier's eyes, completely mesmerized by them.

"I'll put it like this," she told him. "My pussy was so damn wet when I saw you bussin' that big ass gun. That shit was the sexiest thing I have ever seen."

"Well, I guess you gon' be soakin' a lot of panties, Ma, 'cause shit's finna be goin' down."

"Me first," she told him with a devious smile, undoing his pants from under her. "I'm goin' down, baby. I'm about to suck this dick so good."

Xavier's dick got as hard as a steel pipe at her words. Kenzie slid off of him, pulling him up to his feet. She undid his jeans all the way and yanked them, plus his Ralph Lauren boxer briefs, down to his ankles. Her eyes went wide in shock when she saw what he was working with. Xavier's hard ten inch joint pulsated, pointing right at her. Kenzie licked her sexy lips, looking at it hungrily. She pushed him back down on the couch, then she pulled her tight t-shirt off, undid her bra, and let her succulent 36DD-cup breasts free. She pulled her leggings and her thong all the way off and stood in front of Xavier ass naked, looking so damn good.

"Damn, Ma. You got a beautiful body," he told her as his dick throbbed.

Kenzie could see it in his eyes; Xavier was yearning for her. She sank down to her knees and pushed his legs apart, getting between them. She took his dick into her hand and held it, putting her lips to it and kissing all over his shaft. She teased him by flicking her tongue across his nuts before sucking them into her mouth. As she sucked on his balls, Kenzie jerked his dick with one hand.

"Shhit! Goddamn, Ma! Fuck!" Xavier's toes went crazy in his Timberlands. "¡Mamamelo el bicho, baby! Suck this muthafucka!" he groaned.

Kenzie giggled. She loved it – how she was making his head spin. She obeyed though, giving him what he wanted. She gripped his tool at the base, opened her mouth wide, and slowly took him into her mouth, not stopping until the bulbous tip hit the back of her throat. What she did next nearly made Xavier jump out of his own skin.

"Oohhh, shit! Whoa!" he shouted as Kenzie hummed with his cock down her throat.

The vibration buzzed his balls, giving him the craziest sensation ever. She stopped and started deep throating him like a pro. She used one hand to jerk while she sucked. Xavier was bewildered by how good she was. Obviously, Kenzie wasn't a beginner, but it didn't matter. Those that received such phenomenal head before him were long gone.

"Fuck, Kenzie! I'm 'bout to buss, Ma!"

She could already taste his pre-cum. His dick spasmed in her mouth. She suddenly stopped, and she released him from her mouth and spit on it. Kenzie stood.

"Naw, boo. You and me, we finna buss together," she stated, and with his joint in her hand, she climbed back onto his lap and slid her tight pussy over his cock.

Xavier's eyes rolled to the back of his head. Her warm wet tunnel fit him like a glove. She felt so good. Kenzie hissed from how his thick rod stretched her walls as she let her pussy eat his dick up.

"Mmmm, Xavier!" she moaned as she started riding him slowly, letting herself get adjusted to his size. "Damn, this dick feels so good, Papi. I been wantin' this!"

"Go on ahead and get it, Ma!" Xavier told her as he reached behind her, gripping her soft ass cheeks. "Get all of this dick, baby. It's yours."

Kenzie found her rhythm and gyrated her hips while she rode the dick. She placed her hands on the top of his couch. Xavier leaned forward and motorboated her breasts. She laughed and moaned at the same time, then she hissed with bliss when he took her right nipple into his mouth.

"Sh-Sh-Shiiiit, Xaaavier! Oohh, my God, baby!"

She threw her head back and cried out, going crazy from the feel of his mouth and dick.

"Fuck! I'm finna c-cum! Oooo, shit, I'm bout to explode!"

Xavier flipped the script on her then. He switched and got her on the couch, setting her on her ass. He stripped all the way naked, then three seconds later, he had her legs up, knees touching her breasts. He got in between her legs, slid back into her, and went bananas. He pounded the pussy so hard and fast that the couch kept jumping around. Kenzie felt like she was in dick heaven. No man had ever hit it so good like how Xavier was hitting it. Kenzie could just cry from how bomb it was.

"Oooo! Oooo sh-sh... Oh, God! Xavier! Oooo, I'm c-c-cumming! Oohhh, fuuuuck!" she moaned out.

Kenzie exploded all over his dick. She squirted from how powerfully intense her orgasm was. Her legs damn near went numb from it. His grunting and cursing got her back in tune with him. She felt his dick pulsating inside of her. She knew he was ready to bust his nut.

Xavier's balls tightened as he kept stroking. He felt it rising fast. He couldn't bring himself to pull out. It felt too good! Kenzie reached down and pulled him out of her wet-wet. She slid off of the couch, back on her knees, putting his cock back into her mouth. She sucked him like a porn star high off the powder until he exploded, filling her mouth with so much cum that it dribbled out of her mouth, dripping down onto her chest. Kenzie jerked him with one hand and milked him for the rest. She drank him up and swallowed it when he was empty.

"Ho-ly shit," Xavier said, wowed by how Kenzie had really just kicked off the hottest twelve minutes he had ever had in his adult life. "You are a real live freak!"

Kenzie laughed her ass off. She stood up and looked up into his eyes, hand wrapped around his semi-stiff cock.

"You ain't seen shit yet, baby."

She turned around, went to the couch, and bent over, reaching back and spreading her ass cheeks apart, so he could see her bright pink puckered asshole.

"I need a real freak, Xavier, the type that likes puttin' his big dick in all of my holes."

Xavier's dick got hard again right away.

"There is a God! I knew it!" he said and ran up to her to give her what she so obviously wanted.

Chapter 3

JAVI

"And why is my baby sister hittin' up exotic car dealerships?" Javi asked as he and his woman and their dogs stepped out of their house to go to the garage.

"I didn't know anything about it, lil cutty," Danny told him, "but I can almost bet that Eve suckered Power into her little ideas. She and Gloria are already in Indiana though, so it's really too late for me to get on her ass."

Michelle hit the button on her key fob and opened up the part where Javi's metallic royal blue, 1986, G-Body Monte Carlo SS set with twin white racing stripes, sitting on custom chromed twenty-four-inch IROC Camaro wheels on Lo-Pro Lexani tires.

"Don't 'een worry though. As far as anyone's concerned, they just haulin' cars," Danny added.

"I guess."

Javi lifted the Lamborghini style driver door for his woman and the dogs then closed it back down.

"I'm on the way to go see Sol though," he told Danny, lifting the passenger Lambo door up and hopping in as Michelle push started the powerful LS7 Corvette engine.

"Oooweeee. His tanks… they're pretty full too."

Michelle hit the *D* button on the push button shift pad and rolled out of the garage.

"Get at me though," said Danny.

"Yup. Love, cuz."

"One."

"Bae, I'm hungry as hell. Stop somewhere so we can pick up somethin'," Javi suggested as Michelle reached the end of the driveway.

She nodded her head and hit the right on Wadsworth. She mashed the gas and made the rear tires spin until thick smoke made everything behind them disappear. Javi chuckled and looked back at the dogs. They, like him, were used to Michelle's crazy driving. He looked over at her, enamored by her in her pink Balenciaga sleeveless top, the tight, dark-blue leggings, and the pink Louboutins on her feet with her hair up in a high ponytail, pink lip gloss, dark blue eyeshadow, and her diamond Chanel hoop earrings that she redesigned herself because of her passion for designing diamond jewelry. She looked so good to him, and he loved watching her whip his cars. To him, there was nothing sexier than a chick with a phat ass, cute face, and little waist that could fight like a man, shoot any gun, and drive a SS Monte Carlo with a gangster lean that matched his.

While she pushed the Chevy up Wadsworth, Javi went into his email account. He took a look at the photos of what he had paid $460,000 for as another gift for his woman. It was one of a kind, and nobody in the world had one. He couldn't wait to see the look on her face when she saw it.

***

VICTOR

"Motherfucker!" Victor cursed as he again got Diablo's voicemail. "I'm gonna fucking kill him myself!"

He knew for a fact that it was Javier Valdez's people robbing his spots and killing all of his people. Hundreds of millions of dollars in coke, heroin, and pills were all burned, guns and cash taken, cops all over his businesses, and it was still happening.

Brooding hard in his big lakefront mansion, Victor was coming up with absolutely nothing. He had not heard from his uncle, his father was on his ass, and the top killer that had been handling business for his family had gone A.W.O.L.

Interrupting his thoughts, his iPhone started ringing. He looked at the screen and saw an unknown number. Thinking maybe it was Diablo, Victor quickly answered.

"This better be you, Diablo!" he snapped off.

He heard a chuckle as a response before the voice.

"I have been called the devil by some people, but nope, I'm not him, my boy," said a man that sounded like a young thug.

"Who the hell is this?" asked Victor.

"The Muffin Man, nigga. Haahaa! Yeah, yo' dumbass is fucked; you didn't accept the helpin' hand I'm offerin' you to get that bitch ass nigga, Javi, outta the way. You know that, right?"

Right at that moment, Victor realized who he was talking to, and it made him seethe in anger.

"How the fuck did you get my number, cabrón?"

The guy laughed.

"Nigga, you are far from the only one that's plugged."

"Whatever. What is it that you feel that you can do that I can't or haven't done?"

"That list is very long, dog; we ain't 'een gon' go there, but to put it simply, one of Javi's peoples is my homeboy. I can get closer than you easily."

"Who?" Victor asked, dying to know.

"Don't worry 'bout all that, foo'. This gon' cost you though."

"Of course. How much?"

"Naw. I don't need you to pay me, my nigga. My money ten times longer than yours. What you are gon' do is grab work from me because it sounds like Daddy gon' cut cho' ass off soon."

Victor laughed.

"Hold up, wait a minute. You think I need a connect? Even if I did, why the fuck would I pick up from you?"

"Because I'm gonna take over and bump the Valdez family out of the way. You failed. Move over and let a real nigga handle them pussy muhfuckas."

Victor started grinning then.

"I see where you're going with this, my friend. You help me and I help you?"

"Uh huh. Yeah. Call you soon. Make sure you eat cho' Wheaties, Vickie," the man said then ended the call.

Victor curled his lip up. The disrespect was infuriating, but he knew how to play his position. Knocking out two competitors would get him the recognition he had always wanted. His name would ring bigger bells than the Beltran-Leyvas brothers, Barbie, the Cali Cartel, and even the Sinaloa Cartel if he took out the Valdez family and the Suarez Cartel at the same time. The idea had Victor anxious as ever to get to it. He quickly shot a text to Diablo.

You're fired, and you're a bitch. Go to hell, he typed then sent it. He got up, grabbed the keys to one of his cars, and headed out to put some of his own plans into action while the young guy handled his end.

***

JAVI

"Th-Th-Thank you! Shit! Oh, damn! My f-fault!" Javi stammered, trying to contain himself as the waitress brought his and Michelle's food.

The older woman's eyebrow rose up, looking at him as if she was wondering if he was about to have a heart attack or seizure.

"¿Estás bien, señor?" she asked him.

Javi bit his bottom lip and started groaning. He nodded his head at her.

"Mhmm! Mhmm! Mmmm!"

She set the plates with the chicharrónes de pollo bits of crispy marinated and fried chicken and fried plantains in front of Javi and also where Michelle had been sitting. She looked at Javi once more and saw him trying so very hard to control whatever episode he was potentially going to have. She then left to tend to her other customers in her crowded section of the little restaurant.

"Sh-Sh-Sh… ooooohh fu-fu-fuuuuck… Michelle! ¡Coño!"

Javi's eyes closed on their own, and his hands balled into fists. The feeling of her warm mouth swallowing him up under the clothed table had him going bananas. A minute after, Javi gritted his teeth and came so hard that he went as stiff as a board. He felt Michelle still sucking him, draining all of his cum out of him until her mouth was full.

"Holy shit!" he exclaimed, feeling winded by her vicious oral sex skills.

He looked around then. He was totally surprised that not a single person in the restaurant had noticed his woman slip under the table and stay down there for the last six minutes. He loved the hell out of her for the spontaneous shit she did. Seconds later, after she fixed his jeans back, Michelle slid back up into her seat, smiling deviously at him. She swallowed what was in her mouth then and blew him a kiss. Javi shook his head, damn near rendered speechless by her.

"Mmmmm! This looks so good, yo! Let's dig in, bae!" she said excitedly over the food.

Javi burst out laughing.

"Ay, Dios mio, esta mujer 'ta loca."

He grabbed a piece of chicken and took a bite.

***

Javi left a big tip for the old woman before he and his woman left. On the way out, he held his woman's hand as they headed back toward his MC. Demon and Diamond were laid out in the backseat, chillaxing in the sunlight with the cool breeze blowing through the open windows and the sunroof.

Javi took his lady to the passenger's side, lifted the Lamborghini door up, and helped her up inside. When she was in, he lowered the door back down and went to hop in behind the wheel. Starting the engine, Javi pushed the *D* button on the touch-shift center console and pulled off. Michelle turned the music on and took her man's right hand into hers, then she leaned back and relaxed while Meek Mill's *Young 'n Getting It* featuring Kirko Bangz came on and started pounding from the woofers in the trunk.

***

XAVIER

He roared animalistically as he came within seconds of busting his fifth nut. He hurried to pull his dick out of her puckered asshole and started jerking his shaft while gazing down at her phat, sweaty ass cheeks. Kenzie – face down, ass tooted up – reached around herself and gripped her cheeks, opening up for him to finish. Xavier exploded seconds later. He skeeted all over and inside her ass, coating her asshole with hot globs of semen. The feeling of the XXX-rated bliss had Kenzie biting her bottom lip, still craving more of him. Xavier then fell face down on the bed.

"Damn, yo! I can't 'een remember the last time I went that hard!"

"Mmmmmm."

Kenzie turned and faced him.

"With me, baby, we gon' be goin' crazy like that every time opportunity presents itself. It's been a looong time since I've had sex and even longer since I've had good sex. I got so much stored up inside of me that ain't no such thing as quittin' time," she boasted, not at all embarrassed about having a high sex drive.

"I like how that sounds," Xavier told her, smiling at her.

Kenzie maneuvered herself and got on top of him. She looked down into his eyes and smiled.

"I also watch a lot of porn too. When it comes to pleasin' my man, I will know how to do it the right way."

She leaned down and kissed his lips, then she breathed him in.

"And I do mean *my* man, Xavier."

"You see the type of life I live, man. Me, my sister, and my brother, if we have one good day, the next five are normally wild as hell."

"I'm not scared of that, baby. I'm from the streets; I know you are a rider, but I also know that when it comes to my daughter and me, you'll be there for us. You already have been."

"Should I remind you that Nena is pregnant with my seed?" he asked.

"No need. There were women before me, and there were men before you; I understand life, and I'm willin' to accept that as long as you can accept my flaws."

"What flaws could you possibly have that you'd question me acceptin'?" he chuckled.

Right before she could tell him about her condition, the loud crash of a window interrupted them. Xavier right away recognized the sound of the car alarm going off as that of his Range Rover. Precious ran into the bedroom, glancing at Xavier while she ran to the open window next to his bed. She immediately started barking at what she saw.

Xavier jumped up, hurried into his boxers and his jeans, grabbed a Glock from his nightstand drawer, and tossed it to Kenzie.

"Go check on Neveah!" he told her, grabbing a FN 5-7 out the drawer and running to the window.

Kenzie grabbed the gun and jumped up with Xavier's shirt. She threw it on fast and ran to get her kid. Xavier saw the windshield of his SUV was smashed. A cinderblock rested on his seat. He didn't see anyone though. He looked at his dog. She'd stopped barking but was looking toward the right. Xavier followed her eyes, and they landed on one of the neighboring houses. He saw movement through the tall wooden gate that was at the end of the driveway. Peering harder, he could see a figure running to the rear of the yard. They slipped through a hole in the fence and disappeared.

"Fuckin' pussy," Xavier muttered under his breath.

"Xavier!"

He turned as Kenzie reentered the bedroom with Neveah and his gun. He was about to speak when he heard tires screeching from somewhere. Turning back around, Xavier could hear an engine roaring, and at the top of his street, he was able to catch a glimpse of the vehicle that was speeding away. His blood started boiling. He grew furious, barely able to contain it. He turned around and went to grab his clothes, hurrying to get dressed.

"Xavier? Wh… what happened?"

"A bird shit on my windshield," he told her, putting on his Tims. "I'll be back."

"Wait, lemme get…"

"Kenzie, no. Stay here with Neveah and Precious. I will be back," he told her, grabbing his FN and tucking it.

He kissed Kenzie's lips, put one on Neaveah's forehead, then he grabbed his semi-auto and left Precious on duty while he went to catch an angry bird.

**

JAVI

"Yeah, we good, cuz. Niggas thought we was lackin'. Don't nobody expect a Cadillac truck on 30s to be armored," Javi chuckled as he parked his SS at the entrance door to his garage's office building.

"I'm about to put some Rastas on you full time, yo! On everything I love," ChaCha replied, her voice coming out of the speakers. "I'm so fuckin' sick of that bitch ass nigga, B!

On the real, Javi, Victor Gomez is really gon' cry when I get my hands on him again! On God, yo!"

"Didn't Macho say he had a plan in the works?" Javi asked.

"¡Que se joda! ¡Quiero que ese cabrón muera ahero mismo!" ChaCha snapped.

"You think I don't want him dead right now too? Macho's crafty as hell. Let's see what he can make happen."

Javi and Michelle heard ChaCha groan with frustration. They knew how protective ChaCha was over them. She was like a young mother, frantically trying to watch over her babies like big sis, making sure nobody screwed with her younger siblings.

"Macho is a nuclear bomb, yo. When he blows up, he blows up."

"Then all of our opps will be eradicated once and for all," Javi said. "I trust my cousin the same way I trust you and how we trust each other."

"And he has me here," Michelle threw in.

ChaCha chuckled.

"My worries are over now. Yo, on me, if you see even a bird fly the wrong way, fucking call me, Javier. Real shit, yo."

"After I kill the bird, I will. Love ya!"

Javi ended the call then.

"Let's get to it, shall we?" he said to his woman.

He walked with her to where one of his spare Kenworth T800s set with Demon and Diamond trotting right behind them. He helped his woman up into the cab, then after he did a quick pre-trip inspection on the rig, he started up the 525 horsepower Red Top N14 Cummings engine.

While the engine idled and built-up air pressure for the brake system, Javi got a call. On the screen, an unknown caller was displayed.

"Who's this?" Javi answered.

"The nigga that's gon' kill yo' bitch ass," a man said, then the call ended in less than four seconds.

Javi furrowed his eyebrows.

"Who does that?" he asked himself, shaking his head.

Ignoring who didn't have the balls to pull up in person, Javi got Demon and Diamond up into the truck with his woman. In the driver's seat, he clutched into gear when he saw the air pressure was up to 125psi. The oil temperature, oil pressure, water/coolant temperature, and the voltmeter gauges all displayed that his rig was functioning perfectly.

Javi released the tractor's brakes and pulled off, heading for the exit. Michelle synced her iPhone to the head unit and put on her playlist. Jeremih's *I Like* featuring Ludacris came on and started bumping from the woofers wired in the big sleeper. Javi pulled out of his yard and put the truck on the road, ready to go get the load of waste and take it to be disposed of, so he could get back and chill for the rest of the day with his woman and their dogs.

Chapter 4

NENA

She parked her '96 Chevy Caprice bubble body in the driveway of the ranch style home in Zion, just ten minutes away from where she had gone to give Xavier a piece of her mind. Hopping out, Nena hurried into her house, locked the door, then she leaned up against it. She took a deep breath then exhaled. Nena then burst into tears. She cried her eyes out, completely torn up inside.

She was head over heels in love with Xavier, and he was playing Captain- Save-A-Bitch. She had been there for him in every way: mentally, spiritually, emotionally, physically, and sexually. They were friends at the end of the day. They had everything a great couple needed to have in order to work, but no matter what she did, Xavier just would not take the dive with her and wife her up. Hell, they were literally the same, and they were both truck drivers!

What the hell does that bitch have that I don't? The kid? Is it because she's tall and thick? Or her red hair? I swear these white hoes be tryna swoop in on all our men! Nena thought to herself.

Just then, she heard footsteps interrupt her thoughts. She looked up and gasped in sheer shock when she saw him walking toward her with a poker face on.

"H-H-How did you get in here?" Nena asked, not knowing if she should haul ass up out of there, since he very likely knew what she had done, or if she should run to him, throw herself at him, and put her foot down on him being hers and not any other bitch's man.

"Xavier!" she shrieked as he continued walking toward her. "Please! Whatever you about to do, just wait! I'm pregnant!"

Without a word, Xavier grabbed Nena by her throat and pushed her up against the door. He held her there with fire in his eyes. Nena's eyes filled with tears looking up into his. Then, he leaned in, and he kissed her. He pressed his rock hard body up against her, and he made her heart sing. Nena's hands went up to his shirt. She rubbed his sculpted six-pack abs as their kiss deepened. She grew aroused in mere seconds. His tongue parted her lips and found hers. They danced while their lips boxed. Xavier allowed Nena to lift his shirt until it was over his head and on the floor.

Xavier got her shirt off, then he undid her bra, freeing her succulent brown melons. He reached behind her, cupping her phat, round ass that looked even plumper in the leggings she had on. He squeezed her cheeks, then he picked her up by her ass, still kissing her. Nena wrapped her legs around him and her arms, holding on as he carried her to her bedroom. In less than a minute, they were in her quaint little bedroom, naked on the bed, tonguing each other down as their hands caressed each other's bodies. Xavier pulled back and looked down into her eyes. She looked up into his and saw what she had been dying to see again. She saw love, passion, desire, and she saw him.

"Nena," he said to her in a deep voice that got the pussy even wetter.

"Y-Yes… baby," she hesitated, hoping to God that he was about to say those three words.

"You owe me a windshield, you lil angry bird," he told her.

Nena smacked her lips.

"Nigga! My pussy is wet af! And yo' ass talkin' bout a fucking windshield!"

Xavier chuckled, then Nena gasped when he slid up inside of her. Her eyes rolled to the back of her head as his nearly did.

"Th-That's… ooooo… better! Gimme it, baby! Please!" she begged.

"You gon' replace my windshield?" he asked, going super slow, knowing that Nena wasn't a lovemaker, that she liked getting fucked rough, wild, crazy. She liked being choked and slapped and treated like a thot.

"Yes! Fuck, man! You happy now?!"

He reached up and grabbed her throat, still slow stroking the pussy, getting it wetter and wetter. Nena started smiling. She taunted him, talking shit, making him go in on her. Xavier sped up. She opened her legs up wider, reaching around him and digging her nails into his back. She made him go even harder. The more she hurt him, the harder he fucked her. Her climax built up, ready to blow. Her back arched. She moaned out loud. He let go of her throat, grabbed her wrists, and pinned them down. He went faster, pounding her so hard that he made the pussy fart over and over again. Then, Nena exploded, screaming out at the top of her lungs as she came all over Xavier's dick.

"Goddammit!" she cursed.

Nena had always been baffled as to how was it that he always made her cum so hard. She was sure that she could climax from just his touch without any penetration.

"You must think it's over, huh?" Xavier pulled out of her and laid on his side, pulling her so that their fronts touched.

Nena's wetness was ready for some more.

"You got some more for me, tiguere?" she said, calling him what he, his brother, sister, and cousins called each other in their Dominican slang talk.

"I got plenty of este platano pa'ti, Mamita," Xavier told her, then he put it on her so good that, by the time they were spent of energy and cum an hour or so later, Nena was ready to buy him a brand-new Range Rover.

***

JAVI

"Now that is some nasty shit, dude," Javi said, looking at nearly an entire three thousand gallon pit filled with the dead carcasses of animals that had the whole area smelling like death.

It smelled so horrible that he and Michelle had to wear ventilators. They kept Demon and Diamond in the truck out of fear of their dogs passing out and dying. The old, Venezuelan man that owned the waste business was used to be putrid odor. He wore nothing but a t-shirt, jeans, and work boots with a straw bucket hat over his long hair. Sol laughed at Javi and Michelle.

"The bad thing is this isn't what you're taking, mi pana," he told Javi. "Sigueme," he told them.

They followed the older man to a gigantic above ground tank that looked like a grain storage receptacle. Javi saw it had a 7,500 gallon capacity. A few tanker trailers were parked across from it without any semis coupled to them.

"Do I want to know what's in here?" Javi asked, speaking exactly what Michelle was wondering.

Sol again grinned, then he told them what was inside. Both of them went wide eyed with shock.

"Okay… I recant my aforementioned statement," Javi said to Sol then pointed at the truck. "That's some nasty shit."

"Yep. Hey, ya know on top of what I'm paying to have you take it up outta here, I have an idea on where you can take it," Sol said, grinning like a cat that had the canary cornered.

He told Javi and Michelle. They both then grew the same grin that Sol had.

"This is definitely a new one," Javi said, all for the idea. "This is like… Cook County jail shit… times a hunnid!"

"This is gonna be fun!" Michelle beamed, rubbing her hands together as if she was ready to sit at the table and eat up a big meal.

Hopping back into the truck, Javi rolled over to one of the tankers that could fit eight thousand gallons of liquid into five separate compartments within the tank. He backed to the forty-seven-foot-long trailer and wasted no time hopping out to get his tractor coupled with the tanker. He inspected the wheels, tires, checked the lights, then tested the brakes on the trailer before pulling to the storage tank.

"I cannot believe that we are really about to do this, yo," Michelle said as they got ready to climb back out and get filled up.

"Believe it. Bitch ass nigga wanna keep sendin' people at us. Cool. We gon' keep hittin' his pockets 'til he ain't got no more money to pay these so-called killers to come after us."

After Sol hooked the tank's transfer hose to the trailer, Javi turned the trailer's little engine on that powered the pump and started filling. Javi and Michelle heard the muck flowing into the tanker along with clunking and thumping. They looked at Sol, who was standing by.

"No worries," he said to them, grinning. "Nobody did this before. Might be enough to make your buddy throw in the towel."

"Or he'll keep trying and end up as mud himself," said Michelle.

"Either way," Javi said, wrinkling his nose at the smell, "this some nasty ass shit! Uuugghh!"

Sol and Michelle burst out laughing at the grossed-out look on Javi's face.

***

KENZIE

Lying on his big, huge bed, Kenzie was deep in thought about what she was going to do with her life. She had a four-year-old to support and taking a leave of absence from her job as a cashier at Wal-Mart wasn't earning her any money. She was behind on rent and wasn't even living in her apartment since her daughter's father popped up on her and beat her viciously. It all had her thinking of going to school or taking online courses to get into real estate, something she had always been interested in.

She needed to make money. Her daughter needed to have a life, and Kenzie refused to be a kept woman, even if it was a drop dead handsome and rich Dominican truck driver with skin the same color as cocoa, standing tall with big muscles and an infectious smile that made Kenzie turn into a puddle when he smiled at her.

***

Close to 7:30 p.m., Kenzie had just finished making dinner when she heard the alert that the front door had just opened up. Xavier's all-white, Argentinean mastiff jumped up from where she had been laid out next to Neveah, who was playing a game on Xavier's iPad at the table. Precious ran out of the kitchen to the adjoining living room.

Kenzie turned the stove burners off and went to the living room. The moment she saw the 6'3" tall hunk of Dominican chocolate, her heart started beating like King Kong was in her chest playing the bongos. He smiled at her while crouched down, giving his one-year-old cougar killer a belly rub.

"Somethin' smells bomb, Ma," Xavier said.

His smile had her feeling like she was going to melt. She couldn't for the life of her understand how a guy she had just met had her feeling like a little lovestruck schoolgirl.

"I… I cooked… Uh… there's sweet potato and chorizo croquettes, mini corn muffins with bacon in 'em, and chocolate peanut butter brownies," she told him.

"Well, damn! And how is it that you ain't married yet? Cause in my eyes, you the wifey type," Xavier told her, making his way toward her.

"I guess... the right man hasn't come into my life yet," she replied, looking up into his eyes, trying to see what he was seeing.

"Hmmm." Xavier leaned in so close that his forehead touched hers. "I have a trip east comin' up, and I could use my woman and our little lady to keep a smile on my face."

His words made Kenzie smile.

"A trip?" she asked. "Like in your truck?"

He nodded.

"Yeah. Gotta take a cement truck to my people in Pittsburgh."

"Ooo! The Steel City! Hell yeah, babe!" Kenzie said, lit with excitement. "Let's eat first then my baby and I need to clean up to go."

Kenzie took Xavier's hand and pulled him toward the kitchen, barely able to contain her excitement to once again be rolling big dog style with a real big dog to a place she and her daughter had never been to but heard great things about.

***

"Chucho? Why the hell is there a tanker turning in here?" Lupe asked the terminal manager as he watched the big rig entering, unannounced and unexpected, heading toward the shack he was in.

Lupe's voice crackled in his Bluetooth earpiece.

"A tanker?"

"Yes, cabrón! A fucking tanker, güey! We don't have any fuel pumps here, and we only run flatbed and step-decks from... Wait... hold on... oh, shit... Holy shit! Lupe!"

"Oh, fuck!" Lupe gasped, seeing the semi literally run right through the security shack he had flung himself out of just in the nick of time before he became roadkill.

Sitting in the control room, Lupe hurried to send alerts to all the security guards on duty. He looked at the camera and saw them in the break room. They had all jumped up, abandoning their coffee and donuts and ran out to respond to the call.

Lupe looked back at the cameras that were on the truck yard. The tanker had stopped, about-faced, and the driver's door was opened. He saw a man, hoodied up but with no mask, get out with two big dogs and run to the rear of the trailer.

"Chucho! Chucho! Can you hear me, bro?" Lupe hollered into the intercom that transmitted his voice through the earpiece Chucho was wearing.

He looked around the monitors for Chucho. He saw him seconds later, creeping quietly around the rear of one of the terminal's inside yard dogs. He was pointing an assault rifle at the man ducked low, unseen as the tanker's semi's driver hooked up a hose to the rear of the trailer's pump.

"I hear you. I have the guy in my sight, Lupe. I can take his head off right now." Lupe heard Chucho say. "Give me the word."

Click. Clack.

Lupe's lips froze. He felt it touch the back of his head. Then he heard the voice of a woman.

"Tell him to stand down or you're gonna lose ya head right now, mamahuevo."

"Lupe! Lupe! What do you want me to do?" Chucho asked again, pointing the AR-15 at the truck driver just as the guy started hosing everything he could down with a brown sludge.

Chucho got no answer. He kept watching the guy spray whatever was in the tanker all over the tractors he had parked. As he did, Chucho started smelling the most horrible odor ever.

"Holy shit! What is that shit?" he wondered, damn near ready to puke. "Fuck this shit!" he said then shot up and started advancing, keeping his eyes on the man and the dogs.

"Stand down, Chucho! Stand down now!" He suddenly heard.

Chucho stopped in his tracks.

"Stand down? What the fuck, Lupe?! I know you see what he is doing!"

"Hey! You! Stop!"

Chucho heard shouting just then. He looked toward the terminal building and saw all nine of the uniformed security officers running out of the exit door. The truck driver heard them. He turned the hose their way and got them. They all were sprayed with the horrid brown sludge. Chucho gasped in shock as they all slipped and fell all over each other. Just then, Chucho heard growling. He looked back to his left just in time to see the two massive dogs running toward him.

"Oh, fuck!" he shouted and took off running back to the yarder truck.

He dropped his gun and jumped up the cab, making it onto the roof just in the nick of time. The vicious canines jumped up and down, barking angrily, drooling, locked onto him like drones honing in on a marked target, refusing to leave without neutralizing the threat.

***

MICHELLE

"Good job, yo," she told the guy manning the control room.

Crack!

She bashed in the back of his head with her Sig Sauer, knocking him clean out.

"You good, bae?" She heard Javi's voice in her earpiece.

Looking at the screen where he was standing at the rear of the trailer, she saw he had emptied all 7,500 gallons of grinded up humans all over the place.

"Yep. I'm on the way back out now," Michelle said, grabbing the sleeping guard's iPhone.

"Okay. Uh… could you maybe step on it? It smells like dead animals and caca."

Michelle laughed. "Yo vengo, Papi."

She pulled her own phone out and activated the software uploaded to hers and cloned the guard's, receiving all the data for the workings and schedule of the Fast Lane Logistics' Des Plaine's location along with the numbers to key players in Victor Gomez's organization. Without wasting another minute, Michelle hurried out of the control room and out of the building. She ran past all the guards that were hunched over, puking their guts up from being sick to their stomachs. Chunks of roadkill and euthanized animal parts, mixed with tons of gallons of animal and human waste, covered them as if they'd swam in Sol's tank.

"Hahaaa, suckers!" Michelle teased them as she ran past them.

She got to Javi right as he was putting the hose up. She hollered for the dogs. Demon bit down on the barrel of the AR the guard had dropped then ran with Diamond to their humans. Michelle praised them both for a job well done. Javi got his woman and the dogs back up into the Kenworth, then sticking his middle finger up at the man that was still on the roof of the yard, he climbed up and got back behind the wheel.

"Top that, bitch for Gomez," Michelle heard her fiancé say. Then, as he simultaneously released the tractor and trailer's brakes, shifting straight into third gear, he pulled off and blew out the sludge yard, leaving everyone alive but with hurt pride and embarrassment that would forever keep them from watching any horror movies.

***

KENZIE

She opened the orange container and poured a few of her pills into her hand. Taking them, she washed them down with a cup of water. Her confidence was restored right then.

"Kiss my ass, Crohn's," she said to herself, wishing she could just get rid of the disease altogether.

She looked in the mirror then checked herself out. The tight, white, long sleeved, Old Navy belly top let her flat stomach show. With it, she put on a pair of old, stone-washed jeggings and on her feet were white flats. In a full-body mirror, she turned to the side and looked at her phat, round ass, smiling at what so many other women swore was fake because they thought she was white. Her hair was in a cheerleader ponytail, and her baby hairs were gelled down around her gorgeous face. She put on black eyeliner, red lipstick, her silver hoop earrings with a matching necklace, then a spritz of Guess perfume. She looked in the mirror once more then. Kenzie saw something in the mirror that she hadn't seen in a long time. She saw a beautiful woman that somebody actually cared about.

"Mommy."

Her daughter entered the bedroom, dressed in a pink denim jacket and shorts outfit with a shirt that said *Star Girl* on the chest. She had on white Air Force 1s with pink Nike swooshes and laces. Her curly brown hair was pulled back into a ponytail, and little rhinestone earrings twinkled in her ears.

"Hey, mamas! What's up?" Kenzie went to her little girl and picked her up.

"Can we live with Xavier forever?" Neveah asked her.

Kenzie smiled.

"Um... well..." she paused, not knowing how to answer the question.

Just then, Xavier entered, talking on his phone with Precious behind him. Kenzie could hear Javi's voice since it was on speaker.

***

XAVIER

"Yo, I spent some money, bro; we got all new rides to go pick up asap," Javi told him.

"Word?" Xavier asked, looking at the two ladies that had been making his house a home since they arrived.

"Yeah. Put that trip to take that to P-Dub on hold and get all yo' guys and yaself up to the Pete shop. I already let Eve know too, and I don't care what she say; I wasn't leavin' Nena out of it."

"¡Ciño, 'mano," Xavier cursed, making himself not look at Kenzie.

Javi started laughing.

"What? I say something wrong?"

"Ahora 'toy con ella y su hija, nigga, y tu dices el nombre de ella. Chacho, mano," Xavier said just as Kenzie made her way over to him with Neveah still in her arms.

He took it off of speakerphone mode before Javi could bring up any other women.

"Bro, Nena and yo' other lil dips gon' gang up on yo big ass and put some voodoo on you." Javi burst out laughing.

Xavier could hear Michelle laughing too.

"Maaan, vete. Yo hago lo que me de la maldita gana. ¡Coño!"

"Yeah, I hear you, but I don't believe you."

"Whatever, bro. Where's Eve at though?"

"An hour out from Pittsburgh. You all should meet up wit' me 'n babe at the Skillet before y'all dip since the dealership's up that way anyways."

"Aight. Sounds good. I'ma tell 'Good and Pete to head on up."

"You gon' love what I found for you too, bro, but yo ass gon' trip on what I got for me – or rather what Michelle forced me to buy."

"As long as it ain't a Cascadia or that new ugly ass 5700 Western Star, who cares?"

"Uh huh. Te hablo despues, tiguere," Javi said.

"Later, bro."

Xavier ended the call. He looked at the red head and her daughter.

"Well, bro did a little expandin', so we gotta shoot north up to Caledonia and pick up my new ride."

"New ride?"

"Yeah. My brother just bought everybody new trucks, even though he know me and Eve got long money too."

Kenzie nodded her head.

"I might be in the wrong field of work if drivin' trucks get gwop like what y'all bring in."

Xavier laughed, knowing that she had no clue what had them all sitting on tens of millions each.

"Your laugh," she then said, setting her daughter down on her feet. "I don't know why, but it... does something to me, baby."

"What it do?" he asked, stepping close to her with a smile on his face.

"Makes me feel like ain't no way that it's not against the law for a man to be as fine as you are."

He chuckled.

"And it shall be against the law for you to have all that ass!"

Kenzie turned around and leaned over, poking it out farther than what it already did, and she made it wiggle, hypnotizing Xavier with her full moon.

"You mean all this ass?"

Xavier bit his lip, wanting to smack it, but then he remembered her daughter was in the room.

"Yes. That one," he told her, nodding his head in Neveah's direction.

Kenzie gasped and stood up. Thankfully, Neveah was preoccupied with Precious and not paying her mother and Xavier any attention.

"We shall head out though before we never make it out of this bedroom."

"Don't make it sound so horrible, handsome," Kenzie purred seductively. "Neveah, time to go, my pretty little lady."

Xavier watched Kenzie grab her purse then her daughter's hand. His eyes went to her jegging-clad ass, and he bit his bottom lip again

¡Ay, mi madre, ese culo es muy jugoso! ¡Coño! he thought to himself.

"Come on, mamas. You're comin' too," he told Precious.

She barked and wagged her tail, then she took off running to catch up with Kenzie and Neveah with Xavier following.

Chapter 5

VICTOR

"That shit is nasty! What the fuck, man?!" he said once his Des Plaines terminal supervisor told him about what had happened an hour ago. "Who does that shit?"

"Whoever you pissed off, jefe," said Lupe. "It'd be nice to know next time."

"You know working for me comes with a price tag on your head, pendejo, asi que, deal with it and don't get caught slipping again. Now clean that shit up and keep my trucks working, Lupe, or you're fired!"

Victor ended the call and laughed.

"Touché, Javier. I can play the body game too," he said to himself.

Lying reclined in his deluxe CEO edition Cadillac Escalade, he was enroute to meet the young guy that claimed to have an in with the Valdez family that could be used to knock them out of the game once and for all.

"Victor?" called the gorgeous cinnamon colored model that he had flown up from Miami.

He turned his head and looked at her. She was bad-bad. Her flawless skin, her dark brown hair, and her slim model face gave her such an exotic look. The shiny satin-copper colored cocktail dress she had on showed off her runway model figure. She was the type one could put a ring on, but Victor's reasoning for having reached out to the girl was beyond relations.

Recently, he discovered that his father was indeed going to cut off his supply line. That meant no more drugs for him to make tens and hundreds of millions of dollars from. Victor couldn't have that, so he reached out to a few of his friends that had friends in Florida to help him get in contact with the Peruvian belle. Her father was a farmer in Peru and was reported to have hundreds of acres of old school strains of cocaine plants. Through the grapevine, her father, who had never allowed his plantation of coca plants to be harvested and turned into coke but used for medicinal reasons, was ready to get rich and retire.

Many people had reached out to the old man, but none had been successful. Victor knew his daughter was thirsty for her career to reach stardom. He knew people in Mexico that were connected and could get her where she wanted to be, so when he got in contact with her, he made his pitch. She agreed to come up to Illinois and get introduced to the big players of Chicago. Now, joining forces with Marco wasn't so upsetting. He'd kill two birds with one stone then get his father out of the way, and all would be his to do as he pleased.

"¿Si, bonita?" he replied, smiling at her.

"¿Cuando me vas a presntar a tu gente?" she asked, wondering how long it was going to be until he introduced her to who he claimed he knew.

He told her, "Soon," patting her thigh and rubbing it with a smile. She smiled back then overlapped her right leg over her left.

Victor's phone rang again. He answered the call reluctantly.

"Another secretary bites the dust, eh?" Detective Barrea asked.

Victor curled his lip up at the voice of his sarcastic ass uncle.

"What?"

"We found Penelope Cisneros burned to a crisp in her own oven."

"Aw, come on, man! How the hell did that happen?!"

"Someone didn't like her."

"Did you locate Diablo?" Victor asked.

"Ha! No."

"You're about to get fired, tio. What the fuck good are you?!" he griped and ended the call.

"Victor? ¿Cuando?" she asked again.

"Soon, Nancy, chingao! ¡Calmate!" he snapped, pissed that out of everything going wrong, he now had a nagging bitch in his ride.

Victor's two-vehicle escort got off of 94 in Guinee at Grand. His driver allowed the lead van east, passing Six Flags: Great America. They approached Milwaukee Avenue and was just about to roll through the intersection when, out of nowhere, a speeding semi careened into the lead van with such force that it exploded on impact.

"Holy shit!" Victor shouted as the front of the Escalade hit the trailer's wheels and sent it spinning out of control.

Nancy screamed in fear as she was tossed around like a ragdoll. The van behind them was then rear ended hard by another semi. It went flying, landing by the BP gas station at the corner of the intersection. Victor, dazed and bleeding from a head wound, picked himself up off of the floor. Nancy was crying, bleeding as well; broken glass had cut her face and hands up pretty badly.

"¡Nancy! ¿Estas bien, mi amor?" Victor asked, panicked to lose his potential connection to a surplus product.

"I think!" she cried. "I hurt, Papi! ¡Ayudame!"

He saw her foot was trapped under her chair, bent in an awkward position.

"Shit! Hold on!"

Just then, Victor heard the two men up front shout in fear.

Brrrrrrrr! Brrrrrr! Brrrrrr!

Brrrrrrrrr! Brrrrrr! Brrrrrr!

Machine gunfire erupted and silenced them both.

"Oohh, Mister Goooomeeeez!"

Victor heard someone holler his name. Fearfully, he turned and looked toward his window. Standing there was a big, muscular guy in all black with a ski mask on, long braid tails sticking out from under it. He started tapping on the window with a Glock .40.

"Viiictooor! Come out and plaaay! Viiictooor! Come out and plaaaay! Victoooor! Come out and plaaay, bitch!"

Shooting from very close by made Victor look out of the front of the Cadillac truck. As the ski masked man kept tapping on the window and repeating himself, Victor saw that three black Hummers had pulled up and got to dumping on the shooters in the rear van – the few that had managed to get out. The dread heads laid them all down with ease while the first van roasted all the others. The big rigs that had hit the vans had turned around and come back.

"Viiictoooor! Bring your bitch ass out and die!" the masked man yelled.

"Victor! ¡Por favor ayudame!" Nancy cried, foot still stuck.

"Hold on, Nancy! I have to get us out of here!" Victor said and quickly climbed through the partition – where the window had also been shattered by bullets – and pushed the dead driver out the door.

Blood and guts were splattered all over the interior. The two men looked like dead Freddy Krugers – completely annihilated.

"Where you goin', Bitch-tooorr?!" the masked man yelled through the passenger window. "Don't run now, bitch nigga!"

Victor panickily got the engine started just as the gunman raised his Glock. He slammed it into drive and mashed the gas, taking off like a bat out of hell, thanking the Man above the SUV still actually rolled.

Macho watched the Escalade speed off. Victor Gomes now had the fear of the devil chasing him. Macho burst out laughing.

"Bae! Why the fuck you let him get away?" snapped Yessy as she jumped down from the driver's seat of one of the semis.

G-Baby got out of the other big rig, equally pissed.

"Yeah, Macho! What the fuck, joe?!"

"Chill out, yo. It's all good," Macho said as the Jamaicans hopped back into their Hummers and dipped off. "We got his ho ass right how we want him… terrified. Narco did his job, and ChaCha's resources always work."

Yessy's lip curled in disgust.

"Fuck that fat, bitch ass nigga, yo!" she snapped. "I can't believe you involved him in your family beef!"

"He's a snake, Macho!" G-Baby yelled. "Fuck that fat ass mamabicho!" She called him a cocksucker in Spanish.

"You know we should be getting up outta here," Macho replied as they all heard sirens wailing out from not far at all since the Gurnee police station was literally up the street. "We're supposed to be gone by the time the pigs get here; that was the chief's deal, so shut y'all asses up and let's go!"

Macho walked toward the rig Yessy rammed the first van with. Yessy's eyes narrowed as she scowled at his back.

"¡Te lo juro por dios, voy meterle en la cara cuando llegue a casa, yo!"

"I'ma help you beat his ass too," G-Baby said, then they both ran to the semis, hopped in, and took off, dipping to the north on Milwaukee Avenue, away from the scene not a minute too soon as the first of a swarm of Gurnee police screeched to a stop where the carnage was.

***

VICTOR

"Damn! And yo ass ran?"

"What the fuck else could I have done, pendejo?!" Victor yelled out as he made it to Grand and Route 41.

He banged a right onto 41 and floored it onto the highway.

"You could've shot his bitch ass," the man said, chuckling.

"Victor! Please!" Nancy yelled from the back, foot still stuck.

"And you got a bitch with you? Aw, man, how you gon' punk out in front of a chick, dog?"

"Will you shut the fuck up? Goddammit! You talk more shit than a horse's ass, cabrón!"

"So I've heard. I'm assumin' you probably want to reschedule our meeting?"

Victor shook his head.

"How do I know you didn't set this up?"

The guy laughed.

"I wouldn't have let you get away, clown. That's how. I'll call you with a time I'm available if you still alive."

The call ended.

"Victor! I no can feel my foot, Papi!"

Victor skidded to a stop on the shoulder of the highway just as he got to the overpass of Washington Avenue. As quickly as he could, he jumped out and got in the back as traffic zipped by them. He freed Nancy's foot. It was swollen and purple – broke probably. He carried her out and around the front passenger's side, opening the door and letting the other dead body fall out. She got in, and he shut the door before hurrying back behind the wheel and flooring it.

Speeding away, Victor tried to call Diablo again. He'd been calling since the head sicario and his men failed to take the Valdez prince out. No answer at all. Voicemail.

"Dejalo, cabrón," Diablo's recording said.

"¡Chingao!" Victor cursed and ended the call.

"Papi, I need to go to the hospital," Nancy whimpered, distraught and in so much pain.

"Okay, we'll go to Highland Park's emergency room. It's far away, and I've got friends there," he told her. "I love you, Nancy," he lied.

She smiled.

"Oh, Victor! I love you too, Papi!" the girl said with tears in her eyes. "Te amo mucho, Papi!"

Victor smirked slyly to himself as he kept the gas pedal planted to the floor. He had her right where he wanted her. The connect was his.

***

JAVI

After dropping his truck off at the yard, Javi discovered a trio of Hummers parked by the Chevelle. He and Michelle knew ChaCha had called the Rastas in to tail him after the sludge attack on Victor's yard. Javi hated it; it made him feel like a rapper that couldn't hold their own because they had money and fame. Shrugging it off, Javi, Michelle, Demon, and Diamond got out of the Kenworth and back into Javi's SS Monte Carlo. He pulled off, exiting the yard with the dreads behind him.

Forty minutes or so later, up in Caledonia, Javi turned into the Peterbilt dealership right off of the interstate. A salesman met them as they hopped out of the SS. The shock of the two was apparent on his face. It was the same as most people had when a thug ass nigga with tattoos and braids had anything to do with a semitruck.

The dealership was massive and had everything from new and used semis, dump trucks, roll-offs, and smaller medium duty trucks. Javi and Michelle left the dogs in the Chevy and were led by the man farther into the expansive property. As they walked past so many trucks, Javi remembered all the times he, his brother, and sister all loved going to truck dealerships as kids with their father and grandfather. The two had not just given them their dedication and drive for getting the big bucks. Their love for open roads as well had come from Ricardo and Diego.

Javi saw it a minute later, sitting right outside of the dealership's own truck chrome shop. He started grinning at it like it was a winning Powerball ticket.

"Now that is a nice truck," he said, having to admit that about a Peterbilt.

"See! Told you! I knew you'd like it, Javi," Michelle said, already in love with the electric blue and chromed out Pride and Class edition 389 Peterbilt.

"Not a bad way to spend $397,000, eh?" The salesman was happy that his commission check was going to be astoundingly huge thanks to the six million Javi had just spent on trucks and trailers. "How about we get a closer look, so you can see this beaut up close, Mr. Valdez?"

"Sounds good to me, my dude," Javi replied then followed, holding his fiancée's hand.

***

After all was said and done, Javi was now the owner of the limited edition Peterbilt. It was registered and insured under his company's name. Up-to-date D.O.T. safety and inspection stickers were in the windshield, and the inspection report was in the glove box.

He had a new HDTV installed in the big seventy-eight-inch stand up style sleeper with a microwave and a mini fridge. The new cool gel mattress was so soft one could fall asleep on it instantly. A new Cobra CB radio had been wired up on the dash. His new ride was ready to go to work and make money trafficking the white around the country.

"That nigga, Macho, finna talk big shit when he see me in this big bitch right here!" Javi said, geeked, unable to wait to see the look on his cousin's face.

"Why?" Michelle asked him.

"Because I always swore I hated Peterbilts, but now I got one, and this bitch is flickin'!" he exclaimed. "And it's all thanks to my beautiful, booti-full novia."

Michelle burst out laughing. She grabbed him by the collar of his shirt, pulled him down, and kissed him.

"You are welcome. ChaCha says those are the best trucks anyways."

"Go figure," Javi laughed. "Notice how it's only ChaCha and Macho that push Petes while all the rest of us – me, bro, Tool, Danny – all ride K-Dubs? They the Rolls-Royce of the highways. You can't get better than a Rolls, baby."

Javi helped his lady up into his truck, then going to get Demon and Diamond from his Chevy, he had one of the Rastas hop in to drive it back. Javi pulled away from the chrome shop's garage loving how new his truck smelled and how smoothly it rolled. With the dreads behind him, he turned out of the dealership and headed to get to 94 and head south to Sturtevant.

***

XAVIER

Montana of 300's *Wifin' You* bumped as Xavier cruised north toward Caledonia in his black and chromed out 1994 Cadillac Fleetwood Brougham, gliding along I-94 on chromed twenty-two-inch spokes. He passed by the Iron Skillet then, minutes after, came upon the section where his brother and Michelle almost lost their lives.

Kenzie was leaned back in her seat. A sullen look was on her face as they reached the overpass. She sighed, thanking the Man above for sparing Xavier's brother and Michelle. Behind Xavier was Thurgood and his woman, along with Pete, his baby mama, and their triplets. Of course, bringing up the rear, was a motorcade of Rastas deep in H2 Hummers and Escalades.

Xavier was in deep thought as he passed under the overpass. His thoughts were now on Kenzie and Neveah. He wanted to help them. He didn't want Kenzie to need for anything and for Neveah to ever stop smiling.

Glancing up in the rearview mirror, he saw Precious with her big meaty head lying against Neveah in her car seat. Neveah was looking out the window, petting Precious' side. He smiled to himself then put his eyes back on the road just as he saw the big Peterbilt sign at the upcoming exit. Just before he reached it, Xavier saw two black H2 Hummers on big off-road wheels riding in front of a sparkly blue Peterbilt in the southbound lane. Behind it, he saw his brother's Monte Carlo. The Peterbilt's loud air horns blasted as Xavier passed by it.

"This nigga dun' crossed over on me," Xavier said, shaking his head as he exited the highway.

"Huh?" Kenzie asked with furrowed brows.

"Nothing. Thinkin' out loud," he replied, wondering how Macho was going to react when he saw Javi in a Peterbilt.

Xavier led the convoy into the dealership deep as hell. The eyes of almost everyone there turned to see the vehicles riding on big rims with powerful bass rattling trunks entering the premises. It was like a rap entourage coming to do a show.

Parking in customer parking, Xavier got out and unbuckled Neveah, carrying her out of his car. He kept the windows down for Precious to stay cool in the hot evening temperature; Kenzie adored how Xavier treated her daughter like she was his. When he set her down on her feet, he held her hand, and they all headed toward the row of heavy haul trucks already lined up for them to hop in and go.

Thurgood and his woman, Dana, got out of their matte black Mercedes G550, while Pete, his baby mama, Kerry, and their six-year-old triplets, Gino, Reno, and Nino, all got out of Pete's special edition 1999 GMC Yukon. It was candy-painted blue with the Ferrari style body kit, sitting high up on twenty-six-inch Forgiatos. While Xavier and his people went to get the keys to their new trucks, the Rastas hopped out of their SUVs and posted up, watching everyone that moved. A slip up was unacceptable. Period.

***

"Damn. Bro snapped," Xavier said, looking at the glossy silver ICON-edition Kenworth W900L.

"That is a nice ass truck," Kenzie had to admit. "It looks mean and fast too."

Thurgood and his lady checked out the International 9900i Eagle, while Pete and his girl let their young gunners check out the interior of the new Peterbilt 389. All three of the rigs were built to haul the heaviest and biggest loads allowed on the road, and the prices for each one was the same, if not more, than new luxury foreign automobiles.

The salesman came out with the keys to each truck, paperwork, and the appropriate license plates. Xavier, Thurgood, and Pete climbed up behind the wheels and started their trucks' engines. Xavier's 770 horsepower ISX Cummins engine roared out of its shiny stacks. Thurgood's 625 horsepower Caterpillar growled from his stacks, and 635 horsepower of ISX power hummed from Pete's 389. The three did their own inspections on their trucks before pulling off. Heavy-haul trucks had more parts to them, such as reinforced frames and extra axles, instead of just two, operated by air. By the flick of a switch, the driver could raise the axle or lower it down so that there were more wheels on the ground, adding extra braking power and helping distribute the heavy weight of the load. They all had bigger front wheels that were wider than normal, heavier axles, heavy duty differentials, eighteen-speed transmissions, and specialized gauges in their dashboards for monitoring the extra functions their trucks could do compared to a regular semi. The types of jobs Xavier and his crew did, the heavy and expensive trucks and trailers were very necessary. It took big money to make big money.

***

Wrapping up their business, Xavier and his crew all hopped up into their trucks while the Rastas hopped in their whips to drive them back. Xavier pulled out first, feeling like he was pushing a brand-new Wraith. He glanced over at Kenzie, who had her daughter on her lap. Neveah was excited over how shiny and new the truck was, pointing out something new every few seconds. Xavier chuckled then turned out of the dealership to hit the highway and link up with his brother and Michelle at the Skillet.

***

Peek-a-boo... I see you, pinche Prieto, he thought, sitting behind the wheel of his tiny little Honda hatchback. *You all think life is good, ¿que no? With all those nice trucks and big-ticket business?*

He started the engine and watched as the last Escalade in the armed escort convoy turned out of the dealership and brought up the rear. He put the putt-putt in drive and pulled off from where he had been parked across the street from the Peterbilt shop.

When I come back, not a single one of you Spanish speaking morenos are gonna live through what I got up my sleeve, he concluded to himself, continuing to mentally build on his plan of attack that he had in store for the Valdez clan.

Chapter 6

JAVI

He flipped the switch on the dashboard to turn the Pride and Class jake-brake and started breaking down gears on the eighteen-speed transmission as exit 333 in Sturtevant came up. Merging off the highway, Javi rolled down the off-ramp and came to a stop at the light at Highway 20. The Iron Skillet restaurant was ahead of him to his right. He made his way around it, taking a small access road to get to the big truck parking lot that set in between the Iron Skillet/fuel station and the commercial truck repair and maintenance garage.

Michelle's stomach growled as Javi entered the almost full truck lot. The stop and go eatery had some of the best food she had ever eaten while on the road with her man. As Javi searched for a parking space, he saw two of his sister's ten-car transporters parked next to each other, one of them loaded with cars. Passing them, he then saw his Freightliner Coronado coupled to an eight car exposed rack style trailer, also loaded with cars.

"Shit," he cursed.

"Uh oh," Michelle said, knowing who was driving the 132 model. "Did you know she was gonna be here?"

Javi passed it, shaking his head no.

"I would think the fact that she's pregnant, she wouldn't be working; Eve must have gotten soft on her truck breakin' ass."

"Maaaan… Xavier and Kenzie are gonna be here, and they have the little girl with them. Yo, we gotta keep Nena calm. She's pissed that he ghosted her."

Javi found a spot and backed his Pride and Class in. He got out with his woman, leaving the engine idling, windows halfway down, air conditioning on and blowing for the dogs. As he held his woman's hand, the others walked up to them, then they all headed through the lot to the restaurant.

Inside the Skillet, the aromas of mouth-watering food had them both ready to raid the kitchen area. A waiter took them to the seating area. Javi and Michelle saw Payton and Olivia sitting at a window booth. Across from the two gorgeous ladies was the beautiful and crazy black Mexican and Greek Lauren London clone, looking like she was ready to box anyone for any reason.

"Heeey!" shouted the Japanese-Sicilian Olivia, happy to see everyone. "Whaz hanin', joe?!"

"Live!" Michelle hollered, calling Olivia by the nickname she had earned since she was always so live and lit.

The American-born Payton joined Olivia, hopping up and hugging Javi, Michelle, and the few Rastas that had come in with them.

"Hey, Nena. How you feeling, Ma?" Michelle asked the sour-faced Pilsen girl.

Nena gave half a sarcastic laugh, then she turned her head, looking out of the window at the parking section of the restaurant where, behind it, east and westbound traffic flowed on Highway 20.

"Peachy, just peachy," Nena said with a major attitude.

Javi could see that Nena was hurting inside. He felt bad. She was carrying his niece or his nephew in her belly that his brother put there. The emotions of a woman were like algebra, chemistry, and Arabic writing mixed together. They made even the smartest of men scratch their heads.

Michelle sighed. She went and slid in the booth, scooting next to Nena. She put her arm around her and hugged her.

"Cheer up, Ma. Everything's gon' ne aight. You know that no matter what, he's gonna be there for you and the baby."

"And so are we," Javi added.

Nena suddenly burst into tears then. She started sobbing loudly, attracting the attention of other people. Michelle held Nena, doing her best to comfort the young future mother, but Nena was really hurting. Javi and Michelle both knew how crazy in love with Xavier that Nena was. Seeing him with another woman made Javi think about how he had snuck around on his own lady.

***

KENZIE

"We're almost there! Just hold on! Hold on, Ma!" he said, hitting the switch on the dash to turn on the jake-brake to slow his rig down on the off-ramp at exit 333, down-shifting gears frantically, trying to stop his new ICON before skidding into oncoming traffic.

"Please hurry, Xavier! Please!" Kenzie cried, gripping the sides of the seat tightly, her legs crossed, toes curled up in her flats.

The pressure in her gut had built up so much so fast that from the time they left the dealership to come within a mile of the exit for Sturtevant, her Crohn's had flared up horribly and had her in tears from the pain. Her daughter cried next to her, and Precious whimpered, sensing Kenzie's teeth-gritting discomfort.

Oh, God. Oh, God. Oh, God! Please not now! Not in front of him! Please! Kenzie begged.

Xavier reached the light and whipped a right so hard that he came close to tipping the rig. Kenzie screamed just then, feeling herself seconds away from exploding.

"Xaaaviiier! I can't hold it!" she shouted right as he jumped into the left turn lane where the restaurant set on the corner.

"Hold on! This is highly illegal what I'm 'bout to do, bae!" he told her. Then, despite oncoming traffic, he yanked the steering wheel hard to the left and cut right into the inbound traffic lanes.

***

JAVI

"What the hell?!" Javi saw his brother's new rig cut dangerously across the lanes with incoming vehicles rolling, then it shot right across the grass properly line barrier, barging into the Iron Skillet non-commercial vehicle parking lot.

He was about to hop up to go see what was up when he saw the ICON skid to a stop, then Kenzie jumped out and started waddling toward the restaurant's door.

"Bitch!" He heard Nena scream.

"Oh, shit!"

Javi turned and saw the wild Pilsen girl had slipped out of her seat and was hauling ass to the door.

"Nena! Aayee! Nenaa!" Javi yelled and took off after her with his fiancée and the others behind him.

***

KENZIE

"No, no, no, no, noooooo! Fuuuck!" she cried, feeling one poking out of her right as she got within a foot of the entrance door.

Suddenly, the door flew open and bashed her right in the face. She screamed in pain and flew backwards. Her bowels exploded as she hit the ground, filling her panties up so much that it pushed out into her jeggings. The next thing she knew, someone had jumped on her and was flooding her with fists of fury, screaming and cursing at her like a maniac.

***

XAVIER

"Stay here! Mommy's okay! I'ma go get her!" he told Neveah then jumped out of the truck right as Nena flew out of the restaurant and jumped on Kenzie, punching her up a hundred miles an hour.

He ran toward the fight. Javi, Michelle, Olivia, Payton, and the dreads ran out. Javi and Michelle grabbed Nena and pulled her off of Kenzie right as Xavier made it to where she laid, bleeding out of her nose and a deep cut on her lip.

"Get off of me! Get the fuck off!" Nena screamed as Javi scooped her right up and took off with her with Michelle right behind him, hightailing it from the restaurant before the cops got there.

"Kenzie!" Xavier took her hands and pulled her up. "Are you okay?"

She burst into tears then, sobbing loudly. He smelled an odor right then and knew.

"Damn. Uh… dammit."

He was clueless as to what to do. Everyone in the restaurant was either looking out the window or trying to come see the drama. People at the gas station pumps had their smart phones out and were recording, getting it all so they could post it on social media sites.

She was beyond embarrassed. Her nose bled, her lip was swollen, cut, and bleeding. She had gotten hit square in the face with a door, gotten her ass beat by a chick half a foot shorter than her, and her Crohn's disease had gotten her again. The warm mush in her panties had her feeling like she wanted to die and have the image she knew Xavier was seeing of her at that moment erased forever.

"Okay. Okay. Okay. Uh. Um. Payton! Olivia! Come here!" She heard Xavier call out.

The ladies hurried forward as Thurgood, Pete, their ladies, and the kids made it over from the truck parking lot.

"Neveah!" Kenzie then shrieked.

She tried to go to her daughter. Xavier halted her.

"I'll go get her, bae. Just go with Payton and Live; there's showers here, and they got fresh clothes for you. I promise Neveah and I will be here when you come out," Xavier told her.

"Aye! What the fuck y'all lookin' at?" Thurgood shouted at the people recording from the gas pumps.

The dreads followed him and Pete. A few of the people scattered, peeling off from the gas station. The unlucky ones got their phones snatched and smashed. Kenzie was led into the restaurant, right to the store section where truckers and other travelers could purchase shower time and clean off long hours on the road.

Xavier went back to his rig and got Neveah, then he called one of the dreads to take his truck and park it. He carried Kenzie's daughter inside the store, repeatedly assuring her that her mother was okay and that she would be in her arms in a few minutes.

***

KENZIE

She cried her eyes out under the stream of hot water. She had never been so embarrassed in her life, and it was in front of the man she so badly wanted.

There's no way that he still wants me in his life now... I gotta get Neveah, and we need to just get on a bus and leave, she thought to herself.

***

MICHELLE

"Nena, stoop! You are fucking pregnant! Goddammit!"

Nena was still trying to get loose from Javi. Michelle sighed, groaning in frustration.

"Please! Just let me go! Let me gooooo! I need to talk to him! Please, Javi!" Nena cried.

"Nena, you will talk to him, but it won't be tonight," Javi told her, keeping it real.

"Shabba," he called out then to one of Gold Mouth's goons. "Take Nena's truck and deliver her load for me please."

"Ya, mon. Me on it, tiguere," Shabba replied.

"No! That's my truck, Javi! What the fuuuuck?!"

"Nena! Stop fuckin' screamin'!" Javi snapped, so close to being pushed over the edge.

Olivia ran up just then.

"Cops are all over the place, Javi!' she told him.

"Where's my brother and the others?"

"They're cool. The restaurant manager told the cops the girl that started the fight got into a cab and left."

"We need to go," Michelle said. "You're coming with us, and if you even think about arguin', I'ma rock ya jaw! Get cha' ass in the truck and sit!"

Nena obeyed, not wanting any smoke with Michelle nor her boss. She got up into Javi's new Pride and Class and joined Demon and Diamond in the sleeper, catching a glimpse of the Freightliner Coronado she was using as a spare to work and get her money up for her baby. Michelle got up into the passenger's seat, Javi behind the wheel. He pulled off, heading for the exit. Michelle sighed, hoping Kenzie and Neveah were cool, but more than anything, she hoped that Nena would stress herself out so much that she ended up having a miscarriage.

Chapter 7

EVELYN

"Hold up! What? You're pregnant, Nena? Are you serious right now?!" Evelyn got the texts from Olivia and Payton about the whole dramatic scene at the restaurant, pleading for Evelyn to talk to Nena before she went insane.

"Yeah," Nena replied forlornly. "I found out days ago; I need to go to this doctor appointment to get an official word on how far along, but me throwin' up 'ery morning is what made me buy ten different pregnancy tests. They all said preggo."

Evelyn was beyond filled with joy. Nena annoyed her more than anything, but she loved the crazy little bitch like family, and her carrying Xavier's seed meant the first child of her brother would be there in nine months, making her an aunt.

"Oh, my God! Nena! Congratulations, girl! Yo, I'm freakin' geeked!" Evelyn told her. "Where are you anyways?"

"Your brother and Michelle refuse to let me go home, so I guess I'll be goin' to their house. I'm in his new truck's sleeper. Aye," Nena started laughing then, "I made that bitch poop on herself in front of 'errybody, joe!"

"Damn!" Evelyn chuckled. "Payton told me, had a big dumb ass stain on her ass. Good job. By the way, we got new trucks to pick up, compliments of Javi. Do not fuck this one up, Nena, or I'ma put my foot up yo' ass. On God!"

Evelyn heard Nena suck her teeth.

"Aight, man. Where you and Glory Hole at?"

"Out in PA. We parked at my grandpa's yard to rest. We'll be back in a day. Don't let me hear nothin' else crazy. You got my niece or nephew in yo belly. Relax, Azalia."

"I'll try. Be safe. Can you pleeeease tell Xavier to talk to me?"

"Yup. Call me if you need me," Evelyn told her and ended the call.

She then sent a text to her brother:

Tenemos que hablar, bro. Hit my line asap. Please.

Evelyn cut her engine off, then swiveling around, she reached down and scooped her baby pig up. Oinky squealed as she heaved him up onto her lap. Evelyn got out of her truck, which was parked next to her girlfriend's Kenworth in the rear of the Valdez family's largest PJ&D Transport yard out in the Murryville area just east of Pittsburgh.

It was a massive yard. It had everything: a huge service and repair garage, big enough with sixty bays to keep the fleet of four hundred and fifty tractors, trailers, dump trucks, and roll-off dumpster trucks all working and earning. Connected to the garage was a big office/ dispatch center. There was a car and truck wash for employees' personal vehicles and the company's vehicles, a gas and fuel station, also for employees – at a major discount – and for company vehicles. There was also an eatery that provided made-to-order meals twenty-four hours a day and a new hotel for employees to get comfortable sleep in luxurious rooms whether they were working or just didn't want to be home. PJ&D Transport had thousands of people employed. Not a single one was treated like a number. They were family.

Evelyn carried her piglet into the hotel with her and went to the concierge's desk, strolling through the lavish marble floored lobby that was decorated with fine Italian leather furniture. Behind the desk, the young African woman that Evelyn knew very well stood tall and slim with a welcoming smile on her face.

"Evelyn! Hello to you!" the Sudanese girl greeted with a heavy accent.

"Hey, Indie! Long time no see, Mami! How you been?"

Indie got Evelyn's keycard and handed it to her.

"I am all good, 'sees. A pleasa to see you again. Ya woman is already up 'dea waiting for you. How long ya in town for?"

"Just tonight. We're pushing to Jersey from here, then we headin' back home. How's your daughter doin' though?" Evelyn asked excitedly about India's newborn.

India chuckled.

"Loud, but she is my princess. Thank you for asking."

"No doubt, Ma. Well, I'll talk to you another time. I'ma go get some rest."

Again, India chuckled.

"Uh huh… rest… riiight."

"Why you say it like that?" asked Evelyn with a puzzled look on her face.

"Oh, nothing. Catch ya anotha time, Evie," India said and reached out to pat Oinky's head. "He is such a cutie pie!"

Evelyn took the elevator up to the top floor of the hotel. She got off, set her piglet down, and led the way to her door. She stuck the keycard in, unlocked the door, and stepped into the lavish suite.

"What in the world?"

She saw rose petals making a trail from the door.

"Okay then. Glory Hole tryna heat some shit up," Evelyn said with a smile while Oinky ate one of the petals.

She closed the door and made her way to the big spacious bedroom. From inside, she heard soft merengue music playing. She stepped into the dimly lit room and saw her beautiful, milk chocolate Dominican on the big bed wearing absolutely nothing but red heels. With a leg up, posing like a hot, lusty woman yearning for some love, Gloria beckoned to her.

"I been waiting for you, Mami," Gloria purred to her. "Don't make me wait any longer."

Transfixed on the sight before her, Evelyn took off a piece of her clothing with every step she took until she was at the bed as naked as her woman.

"Never fear, mi amor. Evie fucking baby is here. Ahora dame mi chocha," Evelyn told her, climbing on the bed and positioning herself between Gloria's legs.

"La chocha tuya, bebe. Handle your business," Gloria replied.

Then, Evelyn dove down to get a taste of her woman and make Gloria cum hard in her face like she always did. Gloria's eyes rolled to the back of her head the second she felt Evelyn start to suck on her clitoris. Her back arched up. She grabbed her own succulent breasts and massaged them, moaning Evelyn's name in bliss.

"Ay… ooo, Mami… yesss… *comemela – eat me–* Eve," Gloria moaned out, legs shaking, toes curling in her pumps.

Evelyn stopped suddenly. Gloria cursed.

"¡Coño, Eve! ¡¿Que 'stas haciendo?" she demanded to know.

"Shut cho' ass up, puta. I'm runnin' this show," Evelyn told her, then she got off the bed, went to her suitcase, and got out a strap-on with an eleven-inch rubber dick.

Gloria smiled then, licking her lips as Evelyn put the pussy pounder on. She came back, jumped on top of her, then eased the fake dick up inside of Gloria.

"¡Ay, Dios mio!" cried Gloria as Evelyn turnt up and went savage on her.

***

VICTOR

He abandoned the wrecked Escalade a few blocks from the hospital he had taken Nancy to. He made it to Walgreens up at Washington Avenue and Green Bay Road and waited off to the side in the darkness. Not even five minutes later, the pristine 1967 Shelby Mustang GT 500E that had belonged to his father long ago pulled up into the lot. It rolled over to where he was and stopped.

Victor hurried and hopped into the Cobra's passenger side. His uncle looked at him with the slickest smirk ever.

"I see you're still not listening, eh, cabrón?" Detective Barrera asked, clutching the five-speed manual transmission into first gear to pull off. "And now you've got him on your ass, pendejo."

Victor shook his head as his cop uncle exited the lot and headed west on Washington toward the highway.

"Who is him?" Victor asked.

"The bat shit crazy cousin of Javier Valdez; they call him Macho, and he will not stop coming for you until you are dead, Vic."

Victor waved Barrera off.

"Send me the info you have on this Macho man. I'll take him out, then I'll get his little bitch ass cousins and that fucking bitch, ChaCha."

Barrera burst out laughing as he neared Waukegan Tire.

"You have got to be *thee* dumbest person on this planet. Hey. Question for you. What do you want on your tombstone? And no, I am not talking about pizza, cabrón."

I swear to God. I am going to shoot your fucking chin off, so you can never talk shit again, pinche mierda! Victor maliciously thought to himself as he seethed in anger.

He pulled out his iPhone and tried to call Diablo again.

"Déjalo, cabrón."

Victor didn't leave it.

"I'm curious; how is it you know such specifics of these Valdez people, tio?" Victor asked as Barrera ascended an upgrade that led to Highway Route 41 and Gurnee.

Barrera crossed over the highway and hit the right turn lane to take the onramp down to southbound 41.

"Your father and I have been around for a long time. I know the original three Valdez brothers, who their sons are, were, and obviously their sons and daughters. You would have an easier time beating a mob of Triads or Russian Mafia members."

"But we are a cartel, Barrera! They are not a cartel!"

"You're right. We are, and they aren't. What you fail to realize is the difference between the two, cabrón. A cartel isn't bound by blood but by fear, bullets, and rank. A family is blood, no bullshit, loyalty, and love. A strong united family, nephew, will never be beaten."

Victor refused to give his uncle any further conversation. He sent a lovie-dovie text to Nancy's phone instead, making sure she knew to call him when she was released, so he could pick her up. She was his one shot at keeping his status, and he'd be damned if he let it slip through the cracks of his fingers.

***

KENZIE

"I can't, Xavier!" she cried, holding her daughter on her lap in the ICON's sixty-inch flat top sleeper berth. "Me stayin' is just gonna keep bringing drama into your life. Look what's been happenin' since you took us in!"

"Shootouts with a cartel? Visits from punk ass cops? You think that's because of you?" Xavier asked, sitting next to her on the bed.

"Well… no… but look at what happened at Bevier Park! That was because of me!"

Xavier chuckled.

"Yeah, and we fed the fish in the pond so smile."

Kenzie looked at him then. Even with tears in her eyes, he managed to make her smile. She was showered and clean. Olivia provided her with clean underwear, with a t-shirt, and tight fitting jeans. Xavier helped bandage her nose, which had split at the bridge. He tended to her like he was a veterinarian, and she was a wounded animal. Neveah saw the way Xavier treated her mother. She could tell they really liked each other.

"You can't possibly want a woman like me in your presence, Xavier," Kenzie said, sniffing.

"Why do you think I'm someone big in status? I am a regular guy that's just fortunate, Ma."

"Xavier, you are rich, and I am a broke ass bum with a child that I can barely support, and I…"

She paused, unable to say it.

"You what, Kenz?" he asked. "Come on, bae, talk to me."

Kenzie looked at him in his eyes then.

"Xavier, I have Chron's disease."

He furrowed his brows.

"Okay? What's that?"

Kenzie explained the bowel disease to him, telling him how it affected her and how it was incurable, which meant she would have it forever.

"No man wants a girl that has accidents when they're in their mid-twenties. Just take us to a Greyhound and we'll go."

Kenzie looked away from him. Her eyes watered again. Neveah held onto her tightly – quiet but sad.

"Nobody's perfect. So, sometimes, it happens. Okay. Don't you got all your limbs?" Xavier asked her.

"Yeah," she nodded.

"Do you have seizures?"

"No."

"Diabetes?"

"No."

"Do you have cancer?"

"No."

"So, out of hundreds of things that could really make you have a horrible and/or limited life… you're willing to allow something that you didn't ask for to dictate your happiness, Kenzie?"

She looked at him again. She saw the admiration in his eyes again, and it made her feel so good.

"No."

"Okay then, punk." Xavier leaned in and kissed her lips. "Can we get past this? We gotta get goin'."

Kenzie was dumbfounded now.

"Wait. Are… are you for real?" she asked, as he got up from the bed. "You still want me?"

Xavier sat in the driver's seat across from where Precious was in the passenger's seat. He turned and looked at her with a smile that made her swoon.

"Yeah. I do. Now, can you make my new ride look even better by comin' 'n sittin' up here wit' me, so I can show you off to everybody?"

Kenzie's eyes welled with tears. She chuckled, shocked and happy at the same time. Picking Neveah up, Kenzie went and took her position in the passenger's seat, looking at him as he looked at her.

"No more nonsense about insecurities, Ma. Nobody's perfect, but everyone's unique," he said then released the brakes, shifted into gear, and rolled off with Kenzie falling hard for him.

***

JAVI

He cursed as he forwarded the tenth call from her. She was blowing him up. It had been days since he had talked to her and close to a week since he had seen her. The girl repulsed him now. She had some bomb ass head and some super wet-wet, but Javi could care less about the physical now. He had a ride or die chick. He had no need for an obsessed thot.

At the new and much bigger yard that ChaCha had just given to Javi, right down the road from her own truck yard on Kilbourne Lane at the border of Zion, Illinois and

Pleasant Prairie, Wisconsin, Javi had brought his new Pride and Class and parked it amongst all his other trucks and trailers that his drivers had started bringing over from the old yard. Like the other one, it came with a service garage to keep all of his big money makers running. It didn't have a truck wash part, but it did come with its own diesel fuel pump station.

Inside, checking out the office and dispatching area, Javi, Michelle, Demon, and Diamond were getting familiarized with the new space when Angela started calling him like crazy.

"Who is that, Javier?" Michelle asked with a suspicious look on her face.

"Unknown. I'ma be back in a second," he told her, then he stepped out to find somewhere to take the call and threat the fuck out of the thirsty bitch.

***

MICHELLE

She was about to follow him when she heard her iPhone ringing in her handbag. She got it out and saw her play uncle was calling her.

"Tio, what's up?"

"What's goodie, niece? Checkin' on you real quick. Heard you and ya man had some trouble on the highway."

"We good, Unc. They keep tryin', and they all keep dyin'," Michelle replied as she saw Payton's Peterbilt car hauler enter the yard.

"Make sure you keep it like that. If I gotta bring New York out to Chicago, they gon' learn who the real gangstas is. ¿Me entiendes?"

Michelle chuckled.

"I was wonderin' if I was the only one that thought like that, but I got chu'. Y'all good out there though?"

"I mean, the Heights ain't the same without you here to keep creep niggas from comin' around."

Michelle laughed.

"You know all you gotta do is say the word, and I'll come home for a visit."

Right as her uncle was replying to her, Michelle heard shouting and yelling. Demon and Diamond both started barking, ears perked up as they grew alert to whatever was going on.

"Unc, hold up. I gotta hit you back," Michelle said, then she ended the call and hurried out of the office just as Payton ran into the building, looking horrified.

"Michelle! Something happened with Javi!" she said urgently.

Michelle heard the SS's engine start up then tires screeching.

"What the hell?" she said to herself, running to the door with the dogs and Payton behind her.

The second she got outside, she caught a glimpse of Javi speeding off, tearing out of the yard like a volcano had erupted and the lava was coming. A few of the dreads had started running back to their SUVs to hop in and catch up, but Javi was gone already.

"He came out of the garage with an ax!" Payton told her as Thurgood and Pete turned into the yard in their new trucks with their SUVs and more Rastas behind them.

"An ax?" Michelle questioned, going wide eyed.

"Yes! He looked like he was on one, Michelle!" Payton panicked, knowing exactly what her boss was capable of, as did his woman.

***

JAVI
(Five Minutes Prior…)

"Bitch! Why the fuck you keep callin' me like that, joe!" Javi demanded Angela tell him.

"¡Chacho, Papi! ¡Tu me dijiste que me ibas a llamar patras!¡ ¿Que carajo, Javier!" Angela snapped.

"I'm a grown ass man, puta! I don't gotta do shit, and that means I don't have to call you, even if I said I would when I got back!"

"B-But... Javi, I..."

"¡Escuchame, puta! I have a woman, and I love her! Not you! ¿Entiendes!"

Angela went ballistic then.

"¡Mamabicho! ¡Jodete! ¡Tu y tu puta novia! Tu eres un pendejo, motherfucker!"

"Bitch, I will slap the dog shit out cho' ass if you ever call me that again!" Javi swore.

"¡Mamabicho! ¡Mamabicho! Mamamotherfucking-bichoooo! ¡Tu no vas hacer nada, mamabicho! ¡Voy a matar tu y tu puta! Yo soy un real gangster! Bitch!"

"Oh, word? You a real gangsta, huh? Mamahuero, I'll chop ya fuckin' head off and let my dogs eat it, bitch ass thot! Keep talking, pendeja!"

Angela laughed.

"Bitch ass nigga, ven a mi restaurante, hijo de puta miedoso, y te voy a dar un tiro en la fucking cabeza!"

The call ended without another threat issued from the angry Puerto Rican. Javi started seeing red. Angela had just threatened to kill him and his woman after talking the biggest shit ever. He was beyond furious. He couldn't understand it. In no way, shape, or form should a female give a fuck if a guy didn't want to rock with them anymore, he had always thought, and it bugged him that there was so many thirsty ass bitches out there that thought someone owed them anything more than some dick.

"This bitch got me all the way fucked up!" Javi said to himself.

He went to where a metal storage cabinet was and opened it, finding a pair of mechanic gloves. He grabbed them, put them on, then saw an ax inside of a fire safety display case. He broke the door off, grabbed the ax, then stormed out of the garage through an emergency side door.

"Javi? Hey!"

He heard Payton hollering for him then saw the Rastas talking amongst themselves with O-boy, Cadillac, and Black. Ignoring them, Javi ran to his MC, jumped in, started the engine, slammed it in drive, and mashed the gas. He peeled off as Payton ran toward the office building and sped out of his yard like a bat out of hell with murder on his mind.

***

XAVIER

"Hell naw."

"Brooooo! Come on, man! Just call her!" Evelyn argued.

"No."

"Xaviiieeer! Just hear me out!"

"No."

"¡Ay, mi madre! ¡Tu eres un fucking asshole!" Evelyn snapped then ended the call.

"Love you too, lil sis," he said to himself.

Cruising along I-80 eastbound, Xavier was pushing through Harvey, Illinois coming from Joliet. One of his RGN Lowboy trailers was coupled to his ICON Kenworth. Loaded on it was a concrete mixer truck. It was nowhere near the biggest load he had ever transported, but it wasn't the size of the truck that was important but the multi-million-dollar substance that was inside the big ten-yard concrete drum.

Having picked the old Mack R-Model from his and his siblings' grandfather's small used construction equipment dealership business in Joliet, Xavier knew he had more than twenty million dollars' worth of grade A Dominican cocaine in the drum, bound for the Steel City to be received by the Steel City Mafia's second in command. The five hundred thirty-six-mile ride east was easy, all of it on toll roads and turnpikes. The late hour meant minimal state police in hidden cuts, and there were no stations on toll-paid interstates.

Bone Thugs' *For The Love of Money* featuring Eazy E bumped as Xavier cruised in the granny lane. He was still shaking his head at the fact that his sister really thought he had any rap for Nena pulling that crazy shit out in public at a place he and his family frequented and while she was pregnant with his seed.

"Bae, I don't mean no disrespect," said Kenzie, chillaxing in the passenger's seat while Neveah was back in the sleeper laid out on the bed with Precious, "but yo' sister sounds crazy as hell."

"Sounds?" Xavier chuckled. "Kenzie, my sister is the epitome of the word. She ain't got no mind. I can't even tell you how many times Gloria dun' came to work wit' black eyes nor how many times Eve came wit 'em too."

"Damn... wait, hold on... Evelyn's a lesbian?" Kenzie asked with a raised eyebrow.

"So she says."

"She seems really... girly still and so does Gloria."

"They asses are just bored."

Kenzie laughed.

"Wow. What a way to stay entertained. Are the other girls like that too?"

Xavier shrugged.

"Kiara and Jada, you haven't met them yet, got boyfriends, so I doubt it; Payton, the Jamaican chick, I think she like both, and Olivia, the Japanese and Sicilian chick, she all about fun, so who know wit her."

The music cut off just then. Xavier saw that Michelle was calling.

"Yo, whaz good?" he answered.

"Xavier, *I really* need for you to call your crazy ass brother right freaking now and find out why the hell did he just speed out of the new yard with a damn ax!"

"Hold up... I'm sorry... did you just say an ax?" Xavier asked her.

"Yes! A frickin' ax! And he won't answer mine nor anyone's calls! Try him for me, bro! Please! Something really bad is about to happen."

"Aight. Where are you?" Xavier asked.

Kenzie was again stupefied by such craziness. It was making her love Xavier's family more and more.

"In the whip with Shabba, Mango, Face, and Kingston. I'm following his ass."

"Aight, sis. I'ma call bro now." Xavier ended the call and hurried to call Javi.

Voicemail.

He tried again.

Voicemail.

"Dammit, bro. Fuck is you doin' with an ax?" Xavier called another number, someone who was sure to be able to get Javi to chill.

"Dime, primo," answered Macho.

"Cuz… we got a situation. Javi's runnin' wild with a damn ax, won't pick up, and Michelle's chasin' him with the dreads."

Macho chuckled.

"Daaaamn, yo. Lil cuz is wildin'. Okay. I'm on it. You and the ladies aight?"

"Yeah. On the way to your city right now."

"Aw, shit! Yo! Make sure y'all go to the top of the world while y'all there, cuz! Homies!"

"Fa sho. That's a good idea. Hit me when you catch bro."

"Yessir!"

"Top of the world?" asked Kenzie as the music came back on. "Is that like a skyscraper or somethin'?"

"Naw. You'll see. And you gon' love it. Both of y'all will," Xavier said with a grin, knowing the spot his cousin spoke of was such a common place across from downtown Pittsburgh; yet it had a magical effect on a couple or potential couple.

Chapter 8

JAVI

Javi hit the brake and slid to a stop behind Angela's little eatery in Waukegan. All sorts of Spanish food was served there, but the specialties, of course, were Puerto Rican dishes. The restaurant was called Angie's Cocina, and since opening, it had become pretty popular. It set conveniently in a plaza on Grand Avenue off of McAree Road next to a small Greyhound bus stop. Javi had bought it for her, as an investment for himself, plus she was a beast of a cook.

Hopping out of the Chevy, Javi grabbed the ax and took a step toward the back door where Angela's cherry red Jeep Cherokee SRT8 was parked, but then he thought twice about barging into a restaurant, even late in the evening, while it was open, with an ax, hopping out of a candy painted G-Body. He put the ax back and saw his iPhone was ringing. On the screen was Macho's number. He grabbed the phone and turned it all the way off, then going to the door, Javi saw that it was open. He went inside and softly closed the door back behind him.

Inside the exit corridor hallway, it was dark. Javi knew the restaurant wasn't closed yet, but he didn't hear anybody – no laughing, joking, loud talking. He took a few steps, then music came on.

Wow… this bitch is crazy, Javi thought as Ludacris' *Splash Waterfalls* started playing.

He then walked regularly, stepping through the rear into the kitchen/prep area and going toward Angela's office which he knew was the only place music could be played throughout the whole restaurant. As he got closer, light started shining in the darkness. It was dim but enough for Javi to see that it was coming from Angela's office. He cracked his knuckles, ready to break the bitch's jaw for threatening him. Javi stepped up to the office door and saw her.

***

MICHELLE
(Minutes Later…)
Michelle and the dreads discovered the G-Body in the rear delivery alleyway of a line of businesses after riding through the parking lot out front but not seeing the old school. The red GPS dot on Michelle's iPhone for Javi's location had disappeared at this location. But they hadn't been able to find the car until a call from Macho said Javi's Chevy was in back of Angie's Cocina.

Hearing that name had Michelle heated. *He left me to go see the thot bitch!* she thought to herself, feeling her temperature rising as her anger soared.

Shabba parked the Hummer behind Macho's dark cherry colored 1987 Chevy Camaro IROC-Z. The Steel City Mafia goon climbed from out of the driver's seat in a black tank top, jean shorts, and Nikes on his feet. Michelle hopped out, a new FN Five-seveN in her hand with a fully loaded twenty-round clip of 5.7 x 28mm slugs.

"He's inside?" she asked Macho.

"That'd be my guess," he shrugged. "I was waitin' on you to go in. Ready?"

Michelle walked up to Javi's car and saw the ax inside.

"Naw, yo. Y'all post up and keep anyone from comin' in," she ordered them all. "I'm bouta fillet a bitch up in this muthafucka, yo."

***

Michelle's teeth grinded as the sounds of Twista's *Wetter,* featuring Erika Shavon, played, coming through a line of speakers in the ceiling. Hot tears of fury filled her eyes as she crept along, both hands wrapped around her semi-automatic. She just knew she was about to see something that would make her black out.

It was dark, but a little light bouncing off the walls from within gave her a clue of the direction she needed to go. Through the hallway and then the kitchen area, Michelle discovered the light was coming from a room which was also where the music was coming from.

Michelle took a deep breath and made her way toward the doorway. As soon as she got to it, Michelle saw her man's Retro Jordan 5s on the ground, toes up. She gasped, realizing he was on the floor.

"Javi!" she screamed then, seeing him laid out with a knife in his chest and a huge red stain soaking his throw-back "Oh, my God! Noo!"

She dropped to her knees and pleaded for him to still be alive. Checking his pulse in his neck, she felt it. She called his name, shaking him.

"Papi! Please! Open your eyes, baby!"

Javi groaned, face contorting as the pain hit him. His eyes opened, and he saw his woman.

"Michelle."

"Shhh! Don't talk!" She saw a towel on the desk, hopped up, and grabbed it, then she dropped back down to hold around the knife to hold the bleeding.

"Fuck!" Javi cursed.

"Shit! I'm sorry!" Michelle said, knowing it hurt him. "I'll be right back! Hold the towel!"

She jumped up and ran as fast as she could in her stiletto pumps, scared to death of losing her man. She pushed the exit door open with such force that Shabba, Macho, and all the others upped choppers, thinking they were about to have to shoot.

"She stabbed him! She stabbed Javi!"

Macho flew inside with the dread heads behind and Michelle in the rear.

"Fuck!" Macho shouted, seeing his little cousin on the floor with a knife in his chest. "Yo, we here, cuz! Hold on!"

Shabba helped Macho get Javi up. Javi howled in pain.

"Take the fuckin' knife outta my chest!" he yelled pleadingly as they carried him out.

"They can't, Javi! You'll bleed out if they do!" Michelle told him, following behind.

"Michelle! Clean this muhfucka up while we get him in the Hummer, yo!" Macho demanded.

Already having that planned, Michelle ran to find a way to do clean up. She found huge jugs of cooking oil under a prep counter. As she picked one up to pour the flammable liquid all over, two of the Jamaicans came to help. In minutes, they had the place doused, but before they lit it up, Michelle wondered one thing. Where the hell was the bitch at?

"If you're in here hidin' like a bitch, roast in hell, ya fuckin' smut!" Michelle yelled out. "If not, I will find you!"

Face turned on the stove burners, telling everyone to get out. He held a bundle of paper towels over the fire. When they caught, he tossed it and took off as the oil instantly caught fire.

***

"It's okay! It's okay, baby! You're gonna be okay!" Michelle cried as Shabba sped the Hummer toward the Valdez family's under the table surgeon's house, which was thankfully very close to Angela's restaurant.

Javi faded in and out of consciousness, the pain in his chest unbearable. Macho, in the front seat, was angrier than ever.

"I love you! Stay with me, baby! Please!" Michelle's tears fell as she held the towel in place, keeping the blood flow to a minimum.

His eyes closed then. Javi was barely clinging to life as Shabba got to the doctor's house. The staff employed by him were already outside waiting with medical supplies and a carry-board. In less than a minute, they had an IV hooked up to Javi and the knife stabilized in his chest, so it wouldn't move and do more damage. They got him on the carry-board and rushed him inside. Michelle tried to go, but Macho stopped her.

"Nooo, Antonio, I need to be in there with him!" she cried, trying to get past him.

"Michelle, you gotta let them go, so they can work on him, lil cuz!" he told her, putting his hands on her shoulders. "Try to calm down. I know that's ya heart, but Javi a soldier; he gon' pull through. You know how strong that nigga is."

Michelle started sobbing uncontrollably then. The Rastas all stood by, watching, angry as hell. They were itching to go hunting for the bitch. Macho pulled Michelle into his arms and held her. While she bawled in his chest, he looked at Face.

"Was his phone in his whip?" he asked the dread.

"Yah, mon." Face pulled it out of his pocket and gave it to Macho.

Macho went through it and found Angela's contact info. He forwarded everything to his woman, who had connections in an intelligence unit on the base that she and

G-Baby were stationed at. He added in a note telling Yessy to find Angela asap!

"Michelle. We are gonna find that bitch, yo. On my dead homies. A knife in the chest will tickle compared to what's gon' happen to her. That's on my raise's grave *and* my pop's grave."

Michelle nodded her head against his chest.

"I just wish I could take his pain and endure it for him, Macho."

"I know, lil cuz. I know. We gotta call ChaCha though," he then said. "She is gonna blow a gasket about this shit."

Michelle knew it. If there was anyone in the family with a worse anger problem and who was a vengeance fiend… it was ChaCha.

***

XAVIER

"He's okay…" Michelle said no more than that.

"Aight, cool. Put him on so I can talk to him," Xavier told her, feeling the need to hear his brother's voice.

A text from Macho saying they had Javi prompted him to call Michelle. She sounded way past horrible when she answered. He could feel it in his stomach… something had happened.

"He's resting, Xavier. I don't wanna wake him up. He's had the craziest day ever. Hell, we both have."

Xavier sighed.

"Tell that nigga hit my jack when he wake up. His ass got me worried 'n shit."

"I promise. Love you, bro."

"What happened? Did they find him?" asked a frantic Kenzie when Xavier ended the call.

"Yeah, but somethin' feels funny."

A pain in his chest came just then.

"I feel like Michelle's holdin' somethin' back from me."

Kenzie grew more worried. She liked Javi and respected his role in Xavier's and Evelyn's lives. She didn't want anything bad to happen to him. Xavier shrugged, rubbing his chest.

"Not sure, but it has my chest hurtin' like I just got stabbed."

***

EVELYN

"Sssss! Oow! What the fuck?" Evelyn jumped out of her sleep when a sharp pain pinged in her chest.

Sleeping naked next to her was Gloria and their piglet. They both jumped awake from Evelyn's scream.

"¿Que pasa, Eve?" Gloria asked, seeing her girlfriend rubbing her chest.

"I don't know, "Evelyn replied. "I had a dream. My brother got hurt, and my chest started hurting."

She reached over to grab her iPhone off of the nightstand and called Javi. It went to voicemail. She tried it again. Same result. Evelyn then called Michelle.

"Yeah, Eve?" she answered, sounding like she'd been crying.

"Michelle? What's goin' on?"

"Nothing."

"You sound sad. You good?"

"Yes."

"What's goin' on, man? I can hear it in your voice. Where's my brother?"

"Sleep."

"What the fuck is with the one-word responses, sis! Did something happen?"

"Not yet," Michelle said. "But soon, very soon, that bitch your brother was fucking with… I'm going to peel her skin off while she is still alive."

The call ended then. Gloria saw the look on her girlfriend's face.

"What? ¡Que pasa?"

Evelyn looked at her.

"Something bad happened. I can feel it. We need to get back. Fly two of the girls out here to take the cars to Jersey. I'm going to find out what the fuck is going on."

Gloria nodded, and grabbing her iPhone, she placed a call to Payton then to Olivia, ordering them to park their trucks somewhere, catch an Uber to the nearest airport, and get to Pittsburgh, so she and Evelyn could get to Wauk-Town.

***

Hours went by. More people arrived to be there for Michelle while the doctors worked on Javi. ChaCha was first to get there. Tears were in her reddened eyes, and her heart was pounding, racing a mile a minute. Vanessa was with her, equally broken. Tool, Yessy, and G-Baby got there next. None of them could even speak. The call was so unexpected that, at first, they didn't believe it.

The old heads got there then, and all of Valdez Transport's drivers that weren't on the road had come as well, and of course, Jamaica and the dreads that weren't with Xavier, Evelyn, and the other drivers were there. It was demanded, through Michelle and Macho, that nobody told Xavier nor Evelyn. Everyone loved Javi to death, but his baby sister and younger brother would go insane to learn of the near tragedy. As for the trio's mother and father, Ricardo and Roselyna, contact was made by Diego using a secure device that nobody on Earth could tap in order to keep where the two federally-pursued killers had been hiding to avoid being caught and not put underground for life.

***

MICHELLE

ChaCha, Yessy, G-Baby, and Vanessa huddled around the distraught, exhausted Michelle with Martiza, Carolina, and the elusive queen of the Valdez clan, Larissa, talking to Macho and Tool, who were both beyond words. Minutes later, as tension and fear for Javi's life went past the roof, the head doctor came out to them, blood staining his scrubs, face mask down so that he could be understood while he talked. Everyone in the makeshift waiting area stood; Michelle stepped to him, pleading with tear-filled eyes to know what the outcome was. The doctor took Michelle's hands into hers and gave her a warm smile.

"He's going to be okay, Mrs. Valdez."

Michelle screamed out excitedly, thanking God like she'd never done before. Everyone was overjoyed. The women's tears of sorrow turned to tears of joy, while the men embraced and dapped each other up.

"Can I see him? Please?" Michelle begged.

The others wanted to see their kin as well, but they all knew Michelle was who Javi would want in there first.

"He is heavily sedated, so he won't know you were even there," the doctor told her.

"He'll feel that I'm there, Doctor," Michelle told him.

"Let her in," ChaCha then said in a non-negotiable way since he worked for her.

"Alright. You can…"

Michelle took off running before the man could even finish. She quickly found the Intensive Care Unit room Javi had been put in and pushed her way inside. She gasped when she saw him hooked up to machines, one helping him breathe, one monitoring his heartrate and pulse. The large bandage on his chest had a little blood seeping through, but it wasn't gushing out as it was before.

Michelle heard the heart monitor machine's steady beep. The sound of air being pumped into Javi's deflated lung was like a horrible song that killed any good day. She had never expected to see her man like that – eyes closed, hooked up to machines, a stab wound in his chest; it made her almost break down again.

Michelle walked alongside the ICU bed. She gazed down upon him, willing herself not to cry. Taking his hand into hers, Michelle held it, softly rubbing it. His hand was warm.

"I'm here, my love. I'm right here. You're gonna be okay after you rest," she said, her voice breaking as she spoke. "I'll be here when you open your eyes. I swear I will never leave you, Javier. I love you more than life, Papi."

She leaned down and kissed his forehead. Then, she did something she couldn't even remember ever doing. Michelle dropped to her knees and prayed. She prayed a very powerful prayer, thanking Him for not taking Javi away from her and his family. And then, Michelle prayed in advance for forgiveness because she was about to sin… very badly when she caught Angela.

***

EVELYN

After turning on her GPS locator system once the Gulfstream G550 landed at the private airport in Waukegan, Evelyn saw that Michelle, Macho, and Tool were all in the same spot and even many of the Valdez Transport drivers. She really knew something was up because she saw that her grandmother, grandfather, and the other old heads were also there. She and Gloria and the piglet hopped right into the black Mercedes Maybach 62 that awaited them.

"Waukegan! Brookside and Leith!" Evelyn barked at the chauffer. "And step on it! Please!"

***

XAVIER

He made a wide turn to Steel City Construction Inc. at close to five o'clock in the evening. The place was huge. Machines of all sorts littered three acres of land. A humongous repair center building was in the middle of the property. Xavier rolled up to the tall, wide garage door and waited. Kenzie came up into the cab, just waking up from a nap with her daughter and Precious.

"We here?" she asked, yawning.

"Yep. Gotta unload then we're on vacation, Ma," Xavier told her.

The door started raising up seconds later. Once it was all the way up, Xavier slowly pulled inside the brightly lit building. Kenzie saw a row of brand-new machines parked across from a big office space. A big, burly, dark brown skinned man with long dreads and a bushy beard came out with two big Rottweilers, followed by two more guys – one with a tapered mini-fro and one a fade.

Xavier cut the engine off.

"I'll be back in a lil bit, baby. If you or Neveah need me, I'm right outside getting unloaded."

Kenzie nodded her head. Xavier got out and went around the front of his truck. He dapped then embraced the Steel City Mafia goon in a brotherly manner.

"City, my nigga, whaz hanin'? Brought you a nice lil pavement packer," Xavier said.

"And it is very appreciated, yo," City replied. "Aye, y'all get my mans unloaded and take the mixer to the shack," he told his homies.

They hopped right to it without wasting a minute.

"Maan, bro, what the hell been goin' on out there, yo? It sound like y'all stuck in a never-endin' war out there," City said as he stood with Xavier.

His dogs, Monster and Missy, had gone to the driver's side of Xavier's truck where Precious had her head out of his window, communicating in dog with the two German beasts.

"It's life, bro. You know how it is, City."

"I do but beefin' wit' a clown that's fueled by greed is pointless."

"Shit, every time a muhfucka got him where they want him, he slips away by the skin of his teeth."

City chuckled.

"Well, sounds like Macho got him runnin' scared. Cuzzo a wild nigga, yo. Homies, cuz."

Xavier laughed.

"Ain't no nigga like him on the planet, fam. On God!"

Chapter 9

MICHELLE

She woke up when the sounds of screaming and yelling suddenly came. Having dozed off, Michelle had forgotten where she was for a minute until she saw she was in the chair next to where Javi was laid up. She started getting up, Demon and Diamond standing and stretching. Michelle recognized the sound of Evelyn's voice at that moment.

"Dammit!" she cursed, not wanting Evelyn to have found out about her brother yet.

She hurried out of the room with her dogs with her. She found Evelyn out in the waiting area trying to fight her way through the other family members to get to her brother.

"Get out of my waaaaay!" she screamed as ChaCha and Tool blocked her path.

"Eve! Please stooop! Come on, Ma! He's okay, but he has to rest!" ChaCha urged.

Evelyn stopped fighting then, but her relenting turned into crying and sobbing. Michelle's own eyes welled with tears as she watched Evelyn's grandmother, Maritza, and their grandfather, Diego, go to her and wrap their arms around her. As they held her, Gloria entered the house holding Oinky in her arms. Her eyes were red and puffy from crying. She knew too that something had happened to Javi. Michelle walked up to the two ol' heads. Seeing her, they let Evelyn go. Evelyn threw herself into Michelle's arms.

"What happened to my brother, Michelle?!"

Michelle sighed.

"Angela stabbed him, Eve, but I swear, he's good. The doctors got him together. He's sedated and sleeping."

"Why didn't anybody tell me? He is my brother!"

"It was my call, Mamita," ChaCha lied, taking the heat for Michelle. "I didn't want you or Xavier to go apeshit 'til we really knew what was up."

Evelyn gasped.

"X-Xavier doesn't know yet!"

ChaCha shook her head.

"With the stuff about Nena, Kenzie, I didn't think he needed this right away."

"He's gonna go ballistic when he finds this out," Evelyn said.

"Lo se, Mamita. I will take all of his anger. All of it. Diesel doesn't know yet either."

Evelyn again gasped, going wide-eyed with shock.

"Oh, my God! Ximena! Danny gonna be pissed! He's gonna put hits on anyone that ever beefed with us!"

"Too late," Macho chimed in at that, his fury displayed on his face. "The bitch is dead; everyone that ever looked at any of us the wrong way is dead. Nobody lives. Playtime is over, especially for Bitch-tor Gomez," he declared and looked at ChaCha.

ChaCha nodded then got on her phone to make a call. Michelle actually felt the presence of death leave the room as if it went to go find its next victims to take to the fiery underworld.

***

XAVIER

"My nigga, what up, yo?" answered Perry when Xavier hit his line.

"Whaz crackin', cuz? I'm out in yo' hood. Can I stash my ride in ya yard for a few days?" Xavier asked as he merged off of the parkway at the Edgewood-Swissvale exit, jake-brake on while he down shifted gears to slow his still very heavy tractor trailer on the curved downgrade leading to Braddock Avenue.

"You already know, cuz," Perry replied. "I'm at my yard right now. How long you gon' be?"

"I'm comin' up Braddock right now from 376."

"Aight. The gate will be open, bro."

The call ended as Xavier carefully rounded the bend and got onto Braddock. Kenzie, wide awoke, had already saw how different Pittsburgh was from where she grew up. Neveah had woken up from a short nap, feeling the truck going up a steep hill. Precious was laid out next to her and got up as she went to climb up on her mother's lap.

Sync'd to the stock MP3/Bluetooth head unit in the dash, Xavier's iPhone's music played as he headed toward Homewood, the low/middle class neighborhood that was not only where his cousins, Macho and Tool and their father and mother were from, but it was also where their big cousins, Danny and Ricardo, came up and established themselves as heavies in the game.

It was in the city of steel that Xavier, Javi, and Evelyn became truck drivers, all of them starting off with Class B CDLs and driving tri-axle dump trucks in the hully and mountain region, making riding on the flat highways and roads of Illinois feel like they could do it in their sleep. They'd all been drivers for PJ&D Transport until they got their money up and started their own businesses. They followed in their father and his cousins' footsteps, becoming high-level drug transporters and started to see millions.

Less than fifteen minutes down, Xavier rolled through the Point Breeze area, which was nice and mixed of residential sections and businesses. He went through the intersection of Braddock and Penn Avenue and passed through one more little intersection before coming to where the overpass with train tracks and Pittsburgh's own private highway for city buses only was. Literally after going under it and coming out on the other side… boom… the hood.

Kenzie held her little one as Xavier continued up Braddock farther into Homewood. He passed a few businesses along with a trucking company that had been around since Xavier's grandparents were barely old enough to drink. The area's streets were very narrow now. Going through Braddock Avenue and Hamilton where a fire station was at the corner, Xavier now had to use his driving skills as, after passing through Braddock and Kelly Street, he came to Braddock and Bennett Street.

"Uh… babe?" Kenzie said, seeing how seriously small the intersection was and that Xavier had his right turn signal on. "How exactly are you gonna make a turn that tight?"

Xavier chuckled and slowly rolled out into the center before cutting the steering wheel to the right.

"The same way I always do," he replied as he crept the turn, making traffic that was in his way back it on up. "Just do it," he then told her.

Kenzie instinctively leaned back, so he could see his trailer's passenger side wheels in the passenger side mirror. He glanced to it and out the windshield as he skillfully turned the long semi in such a tiny four-way. Once he cleared the turn, Kenzie chuckled.

"Well, go on with yo bad self, Papi."

Xavier grinned as he straightened out, waving a hand of thanks to the respectful drivers in the cars that had backed back for him.

"Why, thank ya very muuuch," he replied, shifting up a gear, now closing in on Bushton Street and Bennett. "This is what I do, baby. All year long, getting to the money, yah mean?"

"You did it, baby," Kenzie purred. "You might have to teach me how to drive 'cause y'all be havin' so much fun drivin' these huge ass trucks. And y'all make so much money doin' it."

Xavier rocked with Kenzie the long way. He'd killed in front of her. Killed for her and she fought for him. But telling the family business to someone not in the circle, unless they'd put in work like ChaCha did, was an absolute no no! He didn't feel that she needed to know that he had millions in an offshore account either. Not yet.

Nonchalantly, Xavier replied, "Work hard, play hard," quoting Wiz Khalfia as his hit song came on just then.

A few minutes later, after passing through Bennett and Oakwood with auto repair businesses on both sides of the street, Xavier slowed to a near stop, putting his four-way emergency flashers on right as an alleyway came up. Kenzie realized that by the way he was running up into the oncoming lane, seizing the opportunity before any traffic came, that he was going to back his long ass twenty-eight-wheeler into the super narrow brick-paved alley. She and Neveah leaned back to get out of his line of sight, so he could see his passenger side mirror. He put the tractor in the oncoming lane of the two-way road, stopping completely when, in his mirror, he saw the trailer's rear was just pass the mouth of the alley. He then shifted into reverse. He cut his steering wheel to the left, pushing the Lowboy to go right. Kenzie watched in the mirror as well, seeing the trailer entering the alley with just inches to spare before the wheels hit the curb.

This man is the shit, Kenzie thought as Xavier started turning the steering wheel to the right, making the tractor follow the trailer into the alley.

As they backed past a run-down house, Kenzie saw in the mirror a large fenced in yard behind them. The swinging entrance gate was open and assisting Xavier in was a very tall, light brown skinned man, holding two puppies in his arms. He wore a t-shirt, jean shorts, and Tims. As they backed into the yard, Kenzie saw four big, huge trucks that were not semis. Once closer, she realized they were dump trucks, some really nice, flashy ones.

Xavier got all the way into the yard, backing up right into the space. He stopped, shifted into neutral, and pulled out the tractor's and the trailer's parking brake knobs. 2 Chainz's *Big Amount* with Drake was bumping. He turned it down as the youngest member of the Steel City Mafia walked up to his door, the two nine month old Red Nose pit bulls now on the ground, walking with their owner.

"What up, cutty?!" Perry Royce said, emphatically dapping up Xavier as the driver's door opened up, and Xavier climbed down.

"P-muthafuckin'-Dub! What it is, yo?" Xavier replied back just as excitedly, happy to see one of the most cherished extended members of the family, who was like a brother to Macho and Tool.

"It's good to see you, bro. How you been?"

Precious sensed the pups' presence and jumped out of the still idling Icon. The pups adapted to her right away, tails wagging, yipping and puppy barking at her.

"Livin' large, cuz, yah mean?" Perry told him. "Every day getting this money, yah mean? What's good wit' you though? I been hearin' a whole lot, yo."

The twenty-year-old was the youngest of the Steel City Mafia goons but was the biggest. He stood six feet, five inches, built like an NBA center. He was a young gunner, a pistol popper, and nice with his hands. Growing up in Homewood, he had become a beast at a very early age, as had all the SCMs and those that came up around them.

Perry was already the owner of his own trucking company, following in the footsteps of the old drug dealers turned businessowners, still moving coke and dope under the radar. He was heavy in the dump truck world, putting truth to the saying, "Doing dirt gets you paid." Besides his dump truck business, he was also a part owner of a prestigious dog breeding and training agency, started by his big cousins, City, Cee, and Dee. They specialized in training personal protection dogs and made big bags of money from it. Then, there was the large amounts of cocaine, heroin, and high-grade loud they moved, checking them millions, plus kicking in the doors of anyone opposing them with no games played.

"A lot's been poppin', bruh, but it's gravy," Xavier said as his and Perry's dogs continued playing.

He then formally introduced Kenzie and Neveah. Kenzie remembered hearing about the SCM showing up at Javi's garage, but she hadn't knowingly met any of them yet.

"Nice to meet you two. Welcome to my hood," Perry said to them.

Kenzie smiled and nodded respectfully. Neveah waved at him. Perry handed the key fob to his Mercedes G-Wagen then.

"However long you need it for, do you, cutty," he told Xavier. "Make sure you take them to the top, yo. Homies, cuz, they gon' love it up there."

Xavier chuckled.

"I will. Where Felicia at though?"

"I'm 'bout to go grab her from the airport. Macho and Yessy just got done," Perry said, "at least with what they was doin' for Javi and Michelle."

Xavier's eyebrows furrowed.

"Sounds like their night continues."

Perry laughed.

"When their nights ever stop?"

***

Back in Illinois

Oreo sat at a table in a rear corner of the bar by himself, watching a group of girls with lust. The bar catered to dope boys and sluts. Out on the edge of Zion, right next to Winthrop Harbor on Sheridan Road, it was virtually in the boondocks. He came out at night only. He was a wanted man. He had sexually assaulted his baby mama, breaking her wrist in the process when he beat her up. He got caught and served eighty-five percent of an eight-year sentence in I.D.O.C. where he lied his ass off, telling people he was in for robbery. He had nowhere to parole to when his release date came, away from schools and parks, so he was forced to do all of his time. Now, he was out, no parole, nothing but sickness in his mind. His baby momma fled Illinois with their daughter when notified of his release. Her father, a wealthy banker who she rebelled against when she thought Oreo was the love of her life, despite his warnings, accepted her and his granddaughter back into his life. He bought them a house, vehicle, and established a trust fund. Neither of them would ever have to depend on help from anyone ever again, especially a man that became a monster.

Oreo had been trying to find them. He felt he deserved some money for her getting him locked up. And to make matters worse, he was *still* a wanted man. Formerly, he was a member of the Insane Gangster Satan Disciples, a Latin Folks street gang that originated down in Chicago then spread about the Midwest when gangbanging was the thing. Now, the SDs had an S.O.S. out on his head with a bounty of a thousand dollars. But theirs were pennies compared to the contract Oreo's baby mama's father put out on him.

A heavy metal rock song played through speakers wired up around the bar. Oreo nursed his Corona after downing three shots of Patron. The cocaine and alcohol in his system had him feeling groovy. Lit. Horny as fuck. He was eagerly trying to pick which one of the slutty bitches in the place he was taking to his spot to fuck whether she willingly agreed to it or not.

He saw mostly white girls. Blondes, brunettes, red heads, all wearing skirts and heels or skin-tight jeans and makeup. Oreo's dick throbbed in his Fruit of the Looms as he stared at a blonde with her hair up in a high cheerleader like ponytail. Big hoop earrings were in her ears, her skin as white as Elmer's glue. She wore the skimpiest, red, snakeskin, mini, shoulder less dress that barely reached mid-thigh. Her thighs were thick, and sexy legs went down into pointed toe high heels that matched her dress. The red lipstick on her lips had him dying to see them wrapped around his cock. At that precise moment, Oreo chose her.

I'm on her, jo! I'm finna fuck that ho bitch brains out tonight! On the D! he swore to himself, still thinking he was a Disciple.

So, he waited. Watching. Plotting. Horny.

The girl was at the bar by herself for ten minutes. Oreo wondered if she was meeting someone, but when she pulled out a large wad of cash and handed the bartender a bill and got up to leave, he figured she was looking for some dick anyway dressed like that in a bar like this.

That bitch got cake too? Oh, I'm fuckin' her, and I'm takin' all that cash, jo!

Oreo got up and headed away from his table to follow the girl out the bar.

Outside, it was dark. The few exterior lights that did work barely lit up the parking lot. It was perfect for Oreo, who was dressed in dark colors. He looked around for her. He heard her high heels clacking on the ground first before he turned to see her walking toward a sleek, white, big body Mercedes-Benz.

Damn! Shorty got big money! She gots to if she ridin' that! Oreo thought to himself and hurried in her direction.

"Aye, lil mama!" he called out as she was about to get into her fancy car. "Shorty!"

She looked at him.

"Sup?"

"What's good? My bad to stop you, but I noticed you inside. You's lookin' so good, a muhfucka was a little scared to holla. But I'm tryna get at you. You leavin' already?"

She smiled flirtatiously at him.

"I am. The question is are you comin' with me, like you know you want to?" she asked. "Or are you just gon' eye-fuck every girl that comes into the bar but scared to get at 'em?"

Oreo grinned.

"Oh, I am definitely comin', lil mama," he said and hurried to go hop into the Barbus edition S65 AMG's exclusive expresso colored leather interior.

She got in and started up the BiTurbo V12 engine, put it in drive, and pulled out of the lot, getting onto Sheridan Road heading north.

"Damn, shorty! This yo car?" Oreo asked as he looked over at her riding with one hand, gangsta leaning hard to the left.

"Yahp. This all me, boo-boo," she told him.

"This muhfucka flickin', jo! Yo ass must be a rich ass, lil white girl, huh?"

She giggled as she cruised into Winthrop Harbor.

"I do aight for myself."

"Sheit, you doin way better than that! This shit gots to be like what? Ninety thousand? A hunnid thousand?"

The girl laughed.

"It cost a lot."

"What's yo name?" Oreo asked.

"Karma."

"Karma? Fo' real, jo?"

She nodded.

"Yahp."

"Oh... aight. Well, they call me Oreo."

"Oreo? Why? You America's favorite cookie?"

"Naw, 'cause I got that sweet white cream that tastes good in yo mouth."

She laughed her ass off at him.

"Well, alrighty then, Oreo," she replied as she came upon a parking lot of an abandoned shopping plaza and turned in.

Oreo's eyebrows furrowed as she rolled toward a blacked-out, 1985 Chevy K5 Blazer that was lifted up and sitting on big offroad wheels.

"You meetin' somebody?" he asked as she turned to the left and stopped in front of the intimidating looking vehicle.

Oreo saw both driver and passenger doors open up and from behind the wheel came a woman in all black and a man – a big ass dude – out of the passenger's side in all black as well. They were comin' right to his door.

"Aye. What the f…"

Click clack!

Oreo froze when he felt the cold steel on his temple.

***

MICHELLE

"Yeah, creepy ass nigga. We meetin' someone; you got some 'splainin' to do for beatin' and rapin' ya own baby mama."

"Wait, wait, wait! Hold up! That bitch lied to you!" Oreo capped, scared shitless now. "Please! Lemme go and I'll leave town!"

"Ha! Fuck outta here, bitch nigga!" she said as Macho opened up the door, then he rocked him hard in his jaw, knocking him right out.

"Shut up, bitch," said the Steel City Mafia goon and yanked the creep out of Michelle's Benz.

Yessy walked up as Macho threw Oreo over his shoulder.

"You good, Ma?" she asked Michelle.

"No. My man almost died today, Yessinia."

Yessy understood.

"Well, we've got someone to take our anger out on until we track the bitch that did it. And you gon' make a buck on riddin' the world of another creep."

"Fuck the money. I just wanna get done and get back to my baby, yo. We was supposed to do this job together."

"There will definitely be more, I'm sure," Yessy said.

"Let's be out though, yo. Time is money."

Chapter 10

EVELYN

"You okay? You sound real down right now."

Evelyn sighed.

"Yeah. I was just callin' to see if you… maybe wanted to meet up? Hang out or somethin'?"

Cruising in her Alpina B7, Evelyn had taken her piglet and dipped off on Gloria once the Jamaican had taken them to the yard to get their whips. Gloria was beyond pissed, but Evelyn didn't care. She needed to be alone, and as the drama going on with her oldest brother got to her, she had pulled over and found herself in the parking lot of the Wal-Mart in Zion. She called Prince after she parked and hoped that maybe he could help to sooth her angst.

"Things are crazy right now," Evelyn told him as she stroked under Oinky's chin. "I could really use a friend."

"Where you at right now?" Prince asked.

"At the Wal-Mart in Zion."

"Aight. I'ma drop my cousin off, then I'm headin' to you asap. Gimme fifteen and I'm there."

"I'll be here, Prince. Don't have me waitin' too long please."

"I'm on the way," he reassured her.

Evelyn ended the call then. She leaned her seat back and cradled her piglet. Sighing, she tried to cheer herself up, but until Prince got there, she couldn't even fake a smile.

***

KENZIE

"Okay, then! This is nice, Xavier!" Kenzie said as she and her daughter entered the cozy townhouse. "You own this?"

"I own every house on the street," Xavier told her, speaking on the twelve other two-story townhouses in the cul-de-sac in the East Pittsburgh area. "I don't come here much, but a house cleaner comes in to keep it lookin' new." He scooped Neveah up just then. She squealed in delight, giggling and laughing as he put her up on his shoulders and held onto her, so she wouldn't fall. Kenzie beamed at the picture.

"How you feelin', Mamita? You hungry?" Xavier asked.

"Yes!" Neveah answered, holding onto him.

"What you want to eat, baby?" Kenzie asked.

"Twizzlers and gummy bears!"

"Um. How about pizza?" countered Kenzie.

"Yaay! Pizza!"

"I know the best pizza spot in Pittsburgh. I can order ahead, so we can pick up and go."

"To the Top of the World?" Kenzie asked with excitement in her eyes.

"Yes, ma'am! Now go get sexy for ya man, and I'ma get handsome for you."

Kenzie smiled flirtatiously.

"You could be in sweats and socks and still no other man could hold a candle to you, Xavier."

"And you, baby, all of the girls! Across the world! I could be chasin', but my time I'd be wastin', cause they got nothin' on yoooouuuu, baby! Nothin' on yoooouuuu, baby!" Xavier then sang out that B.O.B. with Bruno Mars.

Kenzie started gushing then.

"Oh, my God. Baby, you are too much."

Xavier laughed then went back out to get their bags from the G-Wagen.

****

MICHELLE

"Ain't no sunshine in thiiiiis sooong… only darkneeesss every day!" bellowed Nate Dogg on the dark and grim DMX cut.

Smack!

"Aaahhh!" Oreo screamed out as he was smacked awake.

Smack!

"Shut up, bitch!" Michelle yelled.

He looked at the woman in front of him. Gone was the blonde hair, the white skin, the slutty dress and heels. Before him was an unbelievably beautiful brown woman with long, dark, silky hair wearing a black tee, black leggings, and black Timberlands. She was clearly Latina. Oreo also saw a big, muscular, light skinned man with long braids and blue-gray eyes standing next to another beautiful brown Latina in all black. Then, sitting obediently, was a young red nose pit bull, a young rottweiler, and a big ass tiger-striped dog that looked like a pit staring at him like he was a big steak. They all licked their chops, ready to tear him apart.

Oreo realized he was bound to a metal chair, and he was naked. On a table next to the big, braided-up guy was an industrial-sized construction machine battery like a car battery on steroids. Jumper cables set next to it along with a power drill and screws. Oreo's eyes went wide in horror, knowing that stuff was there for him. Michelle saw the fear in his eyes. She knew he knew what the deal was. Macho didn't need to be told. He went and grabbed the power drill and some screws. As he walked toward Oreo, the creep started crying.

"Wait, jo! Please!"

Smack!

"Shut up, bitch!" Michelle open-handed him again. "Did ya punk, bitch ass care when ya baby moms begged *you* to stop?"

Smack!

"No, you didn't!" she screamed. "Yessy! Come smack this pussy motherfucker, yo!"

Yessy walked right up to him and...

Smack!

"Shut up, bitch!" Yessy yelled.

"He didn't say anything yet, cuz," Michelle laughed.

"Oh... my bad."

Oreo started crying.

Smack!

"Shut up, bitch!" Yessy shouted. "¡Hijuey puta!"

Michelle and Macho laughed their asses off.

"My turn!" Macho then announced and got ready to drill.

"Nooo!"

"Shut cha bitch ass up, creep!" Michelle shouted.

"Hey. I have an idea," Yessy said and went to where a toolbox set on the floor by the door of the old meat storage room they had Oreo in.

She came back with a pair of pliers and a sinister look on her face. Oreo begged and pleaded for mercy.

Smack!

"God ain't forgivin' you for what you did and neither are we!" yelled Michelle.

Yessy then put the pliers to one of Oreo's fingers and clamped down on the tip of his fingernail.

"Aaaaaahhhh! Aaaaaahhhh!" he screamed as she pulled his nail off.

Smack! Smack! Smack!

"¡Callate, puta!" Michelle yelled.

Yessy pulled another nail off then another and another. Michelle kept smacking him. Oreo was in agony, but it was nothing compared to the pain inflicted by Macho when he drilled screws through each of Oreo's bloody fingertips. He was hurting so much that he passed out.

Smack!

"Wake up, bitch!" Yessy yelled at him.

"I'm s-s-sooorrryyy!" he cried.

Smack!

"Nobody asked you all that, mamahuevo!" Michelle snapped.

Macho exchanged his drill for the jumper cables. He brought one end up with the copper jagged-toothed clamps and, ignoring Oreo's crying, he clipped them to Oreo's balls. Michelle went and grabbed the two clamps on the other side and went to put them on the battery posts. But she paused before she did and looked at him.

"How could you violate the one woman that you was supposed to protect?" She just had to know.

Sniffing, shaking, crying, Oreo struggled to look at her. He was barely able to meet her eyes. He opened his mouth to speak and...

Smack!

"It doesn't matter, mamabicho!" Yessy yelled. "¡Jodeta, puta pervertido!"

"Fry his huevos, cuzzo," Macho then told her.

Michelle put the clamps to the battery. Oreo immediately felt the excruciating pain of electricity shocking his whole body through his nuts. His screams were more like gagged growling. He convulsed and shook, body contorting like he was possessed. She took the clamps off the battery then. The flow stopped. Oreo was damn near done. Michelle went and took the clamps off of Oreo's fried balls. Oreo slobbered all over himself, veins popped out, skin toasted. He was all fucked up.

"Dinner is served! Demon! Diamond! ¡Dale!" she commanded her dogs.

Oreo was conscious enough to hear and see them coming. He had just enough energy to shit his pants right before he felt the first set of teeth chomp down on his left forearm. Then another chomped down on his right cheek. Another clamped around his left calf. then the fourth set of teeth sank into his side.

He cried and screamed as he was mauled viciously by the dogs. Michelle, Macho, and Yessy watched as their furry goons worked. It took them less than a minute to rip the pervert up. The death bite came when Demon bit down on Oreo's throat and ripped it clean out. Diamond went up to him and snapped a chunk of body flesh from her mate and got her fill.

"¡Buen trabajoooo, mis amores!" cooed Michelle, praising her Sicilian mastiffs for a job well done.

Macho and his lady praised their dogs the same then, with a bucket of water he had to the side, he cleaned all four of the dogs' snouts of the blood. Michelle took out a burner phone and snapped a flick of the dead pervert. She forwarded it to her uncle to confirm the job was done in the manner requested, which would earn her $100,000.

"Aight, yo. Let's clean up. Yessy get the C4 outta my bag. Macho, get that jug with the gas and bleach in it and pour it all over this creep nigga. I want him to burn to the point he gets reduced to ashes and can't even be put in an urn when firefighters hose this place down."

Macho chuckled as his woman hopped to it.

"Michelle don't play no games when it comes to this murder for hire shit, yo," he said to his lady as she unpacked the explosives and got it ready to detonate.

"Do you?" Yessy countered.

"Nope! Not at all, love. Not at all."

***

EVELYN

Leaning against her Alpina with her piglet in her arms, she saw the candy-red box Chevy enter the Wal-Mart's lot sitting up high on twenty-eight-inch rims. When it pulled up to where she was, the engine cut off, then the door opened up. Prince jumped down from the Donk fresh in red Balenciaga with yellow-gold jewelry and diamonds in his ears. Evelyn instantly felt herself getting aroused by how perfectly his smoothness with his thuggish swagger mixed together. It had been a very long time since a man had her panties wet. Prince had her ready to go. Period.

"Well, lookie at who we got here. The Notorious P.I.G., I presume?" Prince said, smiling at the little brown fur ball.

Evelyn giggled.

"Yup. He's my ride or die pig."

Prince burst out laughing.

"Maaan, I ain't never met a woman that keeps me laughin'."

"I aim to please. Thank you, though, for caring. I had a really rough day, and I'm in need of a good, kind-hearted person to keep me company."

She was then caught off guard when Prince leaned in and kissed her. She let him, like she had been visualizing since she first met him. The kiss sparked off fireworks inside her. His lips were so soft on hers. His mouth was fresh, like Winter Fresh gum. Oinky squealed a little as he was stuck between hard chest and soft breasts, but the intoxicating feeling of red-hot desire growing like a wildfire inside of Evelyn made her tune out everything but the handsome man kissing her.

Prince deepened the kiss, parting her lips with his tongue and exploring the inside of her mouth. Evelyn moaned as her inferno blazed so hot. Her panties got wet, nipples aching to be pleasured. The itch she was feeling right at that moment, the type that could only be scratched by a man, had gotten to her brain. It had her make one hell of a rash decision.

Pulling back, Evelyn looked up into Prince's eyes.

"You wanna go to a telly?"

Prince was wowed by her quickness. Hell motherfucking yes he did! He wanted nothing more than to take her to a luxurious hotel room and fuck her brains out, but Prince knew a classy woman when he met one. Despite the fact that he could tell Evelyn wanted to feel anything other than the emotional stress that she was feeling, Prince knew better than to take advantage of a woman. It was just wrong.

"Not tonight, gorgeous," he told her, which completely fucked Evelyn's head up.

Wow... I just threw it at him, and he side-stepped me, she thought to herself, feeling salty.

"Don't think I'm not feelin' you cause I am," Prince told her, using a finger to tip her chin up, so she would look into his eyes. "I just am not the type to prey upon the weak. Right now, something is hurtin' you, and you're searchin' to find comfort. You don't want sex really; you want a shoulder to lean on. I have two of them for you if you want them."

Evelyn's eyes suddenly filled with tears. She nodded her head to accept the offer, then with Oinky still in her arms, Prince wrapped her up in his arms just as she burst into tears.

Chapter 11

XAVIER

"You bogus," Xavier stated as he looked at Kenzie.

She burst out laughing.

"Why am I bogus. babe?"

Kenzie had on a tiny, red, tube top with purple stars and fireworks exploding. A deep 'V' cleavage hue gave off an exquisite view of the top of her succulent 36DD cups. The short sleeves allowed her tattooed arms to be seen. With the skimpy little top, Kenzie had on a little purple suede mini skirt, her legs freshly shaved and oiled up, and on her feet were red stilettos with painted toes and ankle straps.

Her hair was styled with mousse for the wet look. Purple eyeshadow, glossy red lipstick, hoop earrings. She was looking so good that even Jesus Christ would look twice, even with her cut lip and bandaged nose.

"Lookin' that good 'n shit," Xavier told her just as Neveah ran into the bedroom wearing a denim jacket and skirt outfit with denim Air Force Ones, her hair in two pigtails. Precious was right behind her.

"It's gon' be too damn hard to keep my hands off of you."

Kenzie grinned.

"I know."

***

Xavier got Neveah and Precious situated in the back of the vehicle. Kenzie sat shotgun. Xavier hopped behind the wheel and pulled off, making his way down to the Forest Hills area, getting onto Ardmore Boulevard and heading toward Wilkinsburg. Feeling so relaxed being some place so new to her, Kenzie no longer felt any apprehension. Her daughter was happy and cared for and so was she. She had a man now. A real man. The classic hit *Love You Down* by Ready For the World came on. Xaiver reached over and took Kenzie's left hand with his right. She smiled over at him when he kissed it then continued holding onto it.

In Squirrell Hill, Xavier made his way to Mineo's Pizza on Murray Avenue to pick up their pizza. He made it just in time before they closed, then he got onto the Parkway to head toward downtown Pittsburgh. From near the downtown area, he went over a bridge crossing the wide deep Monongahela River and cut a right turn going up a long, steep hill until he reached the top of Mount Washington. After one last left turn, Xavier pulled up to the overlook.

Kenzie could already see why Xavier and his people called it the top of the world. They were so high up that they could see the whole city of Pittsburgh.

"Babe, this is dope!" Kenzie said, though the real view would be from the big, circular viewing pads at the edge.

"I said the same thing my first time here when I was a shorty." Xavier turned around to Neveah, who was sitting back, kicking her legs, waiting to get out.

"Wanna see something exciting, little lady?"

"Yes!" Neveah shouted, eager to see where they were.

"Okay. But ya gotta close your eyes," Xavier told her.

Neveah did, then they both hurried out and got her and Precious across the street and onto a viewing pad. Kenzie counted down from three then told her little one to open her eyes.

"Woooooow!" Neveah hollered, amazed by what she saw.

From so high up, the toddler saw a big river then on the other side a highway filled with white lights and red ones going in two different ways. Beyond it, tall buildings lit up with lights, enhancing the city's attractive structuring. She could even see where the Monongahela River met the Ohio and the Allegheny River. Sitting on the other side of the three rivers' merge point was the big Carnegie Science Museum with the casino close by and the famous Pittsburgh Steeler's stadium.

Kenzie was indeed wowed by the view herself, but at that moment, it was all about her daughter's happiness. Xavier held the little one, so he could point out certain things and tell her what they were. Precious sat next to Kenzie's leg, obediently staying put without even being told to.

"This is crazy to say, babe, but it feels kind of… magical… bein' up here," Kenzie said as a cool breeze blew.

"It does, right? What you think, baby girl?" Xavier asked Neveah. "Does it feel magical up here?"

"Yes! I like how it looks, Daddy."

Kenzie gasped.

"Oh, my…"

Xavier smiled though. He didn't mind that at all. If she saw him as that, then he would step up and be that, as much as she wanted and as much as she needed. He looked at Kenzie as Neveah yawned and laid her head on his chest.

"Somebody's tired," he said softly and started rocking her.

He adored Neveah so much. She made him wish he had kids already. Suddenly, Nena popped up into his head. Kenzie saw the happiness in his face fade.

"What's wrong?"

"Nena," was all he said.

She understood.

"Yeah," she sighed, not knowing what else to say.

From inside her faux leather handbag, Kenzie's iPhone started ringing. She pulled it out and saw a blocked number.

118

She ignored it and was about to tuck it back in when it rang again.

"Who the hell is calling me blocked?" she wondered as it rang.

"Answer it and see," Xavier said, holding the now sleeping angel.

Kenzie answered. "Hello?"

Silence. No sound at all. Then, the call ended.

"Asshole," she called whoever it was.

Then, a text came through the phone. Kenzie opened it up then was horrified by what she read.

"Bae? What is it?" Xavier asked, eyebrows furrowed up, seeing the terrified expression she had.

Kenzie held the phone up, so he could see the screen. He read it.

You are dead, bitch! DEAD!

***

EVELYN

Evelyn stood in the kitchen in her big, four-bedroom house out in Gurnee, not far from Six Flags: Great America. In her email account, she stared in awe at a contract worth five million to be a private transporter for three very exclusive aftermarket vehicle buildings over in Germany that only did Mercedez-Benz. It was to make her auto-hauling division the primary carrier for them for every vehicle they had imported to the United States from Germany. None of the cars and SUVs were less than $100,000. The work would bind her for one year with anticipated vehicles per month to be picked up from the Hersey docks. It was all negotiated for her by her father.

Evelyn was extremely grateful for it. The money wasn't why because she was caked up to the max. It was because her father trusted her to handle such a big job. It meant a lot to her. Instructions inside told her to sign it, take the flick of it, and email it to the email address provided. The two companies would then lock her in and issue half of the money up front. As she did, Gloria entered the house, finally arriving home from the new yard. She immediately went to her lady.

"¿Que pasa, amor? Why you just leave me like that?" Gloria asked as Oinky trotted into the kitchen.

"I needed to be alone for a little bit, Gloria. Don't start buggin'." Evelyn then showed her girlfriend the contract.

"¡¿Dios mio! ¿En serio?" Gloria asked in disbelief.

"Yes, seriously. We finna expand. By the time Javi can move around, you and I will have made Valdez Transport's auto-transport division the preferred pick by all the million-dollar car builders."

Gloria scooped Oinky up, making him snort happily in her arms.

"Let's give Xavier and his crew some competition and, in the process, make Javi proud of us."

"Let's," Evelyn agreed, excited for the chance to once again make her oldest brother happy as hell that he brought her on and gave her a seat at the boss' table.

***

MICHELLE

Michelle laid at Javi's side after taking a long, hot shower to cleanse her recent job off of her. Being a hitwoman was fun to her, and it paid so good to eliminate creeps and other low-life clowns, but her passion was in diamond jewelry designing. Out of her past six jobs, she'd been saving up to buy her own diamonds along with a surplus of yellow-gold, white-gold, pink-gold, silver, sapphires, and all sorts of rare stones. She knew she also needed the equipment to melt down her gold and molds to re-shape it into chains, necklaces, charms, and pendants. Plans to do diamond rings, bracelets, watches, earrings, nose rings, and any other type of drip one could wear were going to put her on the map.

Holding her iPhone up, Michelle studied her notes that she'd jotted down about her future business every so often. Her screen then changed as a call from Jada came in. Michelle wondered why one of Evelyn's drivers was calling her, but as co-owner of Valdez Transport, she was obligated to step up in Javi's place during his down time.

"Hey, Jay. What's up?"

"Hi, Michelle. I'm sorry 'ta botha you," the Alabama born twin said with a southern twang in her voice, "but Javi had me go 'n get this vehicle from New 'Yok, an' it ain't goin' 'ta no 'bizness. Evie tol' me to call you up 'n see what 'ta do with it."

"Javi never told you where it's goin'?" Michelle asked.

"Nuh uh. I actually thank he bought it cause the registration says his name on it."

"That wouldn't surprise me," Michelle chuckled. "His ass is always buyin' new cars. I guess you can just take it to the yard. I'll drive it home for him."

"A'right. Talk ta ya later, and when he wake up, tell 'im we's finna beat him up fa' scarin' us all like 'at."

Michelle laughed.

"Y'all can get him after I do."

"Cool. Keep yo head up, Momma."

The call ended then. Michelle sighed then got back to looking at her business plan notes.

"You gon' beat my ass for real, baby?"

Michelle gasped when she heard Javi's voice. She turned around and saw his eyes trying to open up. She grew emotional then, eyes welling with tears.

"Papi! Oh, my God, you're okay!"

She gently got as close to him as she could.

"You scared the shit out of us, yo! For real! What the heck were you thinking?"

"I was thinkin' that bitch talked crazy to the wrong one," he said then cleared his dry throat.

Michelle got up and went to get a fruity flavored Pedialyte juice pack from the fridge that looked like a Capri Sun juice. She put the little straw into the foil hole then held the body fluid replenishing drink to his lips. Javi sipped it until his whistle was wet enough for him.

"Did anybody get her?" he then asked.

Michelle shook her head.

"She took off. Yessy's been trying to track her, but her phone must have been cut off or dumped."

She saw Javi's jaw muscles clench in anger.

"I'ma strangle that bitch for stabbin' me."

"Not if I chop her up with my machete first," Michelle said. "Hey? Jada said you had her go pick up some vehicle but never told her where it's going."

Javi grinned then.

"It's goin' to you, bae."

"Um… but I have too many cars already, Javi."

He chuckled.

"You ain't got one like this, amor," he stated. "Nobody does," he said then attempted to sit up.

Immediately, pain exploded in his chest. He yelped in agony.

"¡Ay, no! Javier! Lay your ass back down before you pop your damn stitches!"

Michelle gently made him lay back down. Javi got pissed from the pain and being laid up.

"¡Lo juro por fucking Dios!" he growled. "When I catch that bitch, on God, she gon' wish she was never born!"

"I know, baby, I know." Michelle got on the bed and laid next to him. "Don't think about her right now though. I have something way more important for you than that ho."

Javi looked at her.

"Dime, amor."

She started smiling at him before taking his hand and placing it on her stomach. Javi furrowed his brows in confusion, but almost ten seconds later, it did hit him.

"¡Diablos!" he gasped. "You're... pregnant!"

Michelle nodded, her smile growing bigger. "Six weeks. I found out while I was still in Texas, so it's seven weeks now."

"Holy f... oow!"

"Javi! Relax!" She chuckled at his excitement. "Dios mio, Papi, you're gonna really hurt yourself."

"I can't help it! I'm fucking geeked, bae! I'ma be a... aye... hold up! Hold up!" His smile fell. "Yo, you was doin' all that gangsta shit while you got my baby inside yo stomach, Michelle?"

"Uh un, nigga, don't do that. I told ya ass what it was when we met; I'ma gangsta bitch 'til I die, even if I get preggo," she reminded him. "Now hush and kiss me!"

She scooted up and pressed her lips to his. Javi's tongue met hers when their lips parted. Michelle slid over and re-positioned herself on top of him. Their kiss continued, heating up as the passion between them rose. Michelle felt her panties getting so wet, feeling his rock harden up under her. She wanted it inside of her, but she feared hurting him, especially since they got so wild. She pulled back before she lost her sense of self-control.

"Coño, Mamita, you got a nigga on bone! ¡Damela, mami!"

Michelle laughed.

"Nope. I don't wanna hurt you, baby."

"Fuck that! Pain is love! Come on! I need some tuto!" he pleaded as he gripped and squeezed her ass cheeks.

"No, Javier," she resisted. "Buut," she then said with a seductive look in her eyes, "I will help you out a lil bit, so you ain't all frustrated 'n shit."

Then, she slid off of him, taking his sweats and boxer briefs with her, freeing his throbbing cock. Javi watched with glee as Michelle wrapped her lips around his dick and started sucking on it like it was a lollipop. He groaned, toes curling, balls tingling, feeling her warm mouth all over his joint. She sucked on the tip then let go, running her tongue down the side to his balls. She kissed them then sucked on them. He went apeshit with bliss. Michelle made her way back to the tip and deep-throated him, going balls deep, making it touch the back of her throat. When she went back to the tip, she gripped it with one hand and started jerking his cock while she sucked. Javi cursed and groaned as Michelle went crazy on him.

"Fuck! Goddammit!" he cursed.

Michelle kept her head game strong until Javi shouted he was about to bust his nut. She jerked his cock and continued sucking until he filled her mouth with hot globs of semen. She spit it all out on his flat stomach, then like a kitten, she lapped his cum back up and swallowed it.

"Shit!" Javi shouted when he was empty.

A knock on the door came just then.

"Is everything okay in there?" one of Javi's nurses asked from the other side of the door.

"Go away! Ow!" Javi yelled, regretting it afterwards when chest pains exploded.

"Javi, don't be rude," Michelle said, then she hollered to the nurse that they were fine.

Javi shook his head.

"Bitch stabs me, and I can't get no pussy? Demon and Diamond getting some char-broiled pork chops when I get that bitch, yo. On Uncle Pedro and Tammy!"

Chapter 12

DAYS LATER

On a warm evening, Javi had Michelle drive him to the yard, rolling with his dread head posse along with Macho, Tool, Yessy, G-Baby, Evelyn, Gloria, ChaCha, and the ol' heads. They'd all had a big dinner together at Macho and Yessy's house, then Javi told Michelle that there was something he had for her.

In her exclusive drop-top Aston Martin DB9 Volante, Michelle turned into the yard, parking at the entrance door of the office. Javi got out, his chest wound tender still, but no prescription opioid pain killers were going into his body. He was toughing it out like a man. Macho had come up to assist his younger cousin, dressed in a Ferragamo fit, hair freshly braided, diamonds in his ears, and diamonds in the Richard Mille on his wrist, swagging so hard like Javi, Tool, and their grandfathers, while the women all looked like queens, draped in beautiful dresses, minimal make-up, and jewelry as well.

"You gon' treat me like I'm an ol' man now, cuzzo?" Javi asked jokingly as Macho put his arm over his shoulder.

"Yup," Macho simply replied as everyone entered the building.

From the office, they went out into the eight service bay area; all of the bays were long and wide enough to fit a full tractor-trailer inside along with everything needed to maintain or repair it. Javi's Peterbilt 389 Pride and Class was parked in the first bay. He took his woman by the hand and led her around the front of the shiny blue rig to the second bay.

Michelle saw the exclusive, brand-new Mercedes-Benz SUV there. Its exquisite Designo Mystic red paint, a maroon wine color, flicked so hard in the garage's overhead lights. The chrome trim and the chrome lips of the twenty-four-inch Forgiatos, faces of the custom ordered rims painted to match the truck, gleamed like mirrors. All the windows were tinted with the darkest limo tint available. There were custom bumpers, side skirts, and dual-tipped exhaust pipes that jutted out from under both rear driver's side and the passenger's doors in front of the rear wheels. Michelle also noticed a "B" emblem in the center of the grill; she knew all too well that it stood for Brabus.

"Wow! On, my God, yo, this is mine?" she asked in shock.

Javi grinned, loving her reaction. There was nothing he wouldn't do to make her smile – from spending a million on a gift for her to putting his face between her plump booty cheeks. He cared about his woman in the deepest way, but the nearly half million-dollar SUV wasn't how he planned to prove it that evening.

Michelle was led closer by Javi while the others took flicks with their phones to capture the moment. She then saw the BiTurbo V12 emblem at the front driver's side wheel fender.

"This has a V12?" she asked, only knowing that type of Mercedes truck to have V8 engines, some with six-cylinders over in Europe.

"It's the new G65 AMG," Javi told her. "Brabus-edition. Fuck 600 horsepower; this joint got 800 under the hood, a little more in torque."

He opened the front door for her and revealed the custom black Naooa leather interior accented in Designo Mysti Red, wood trim, a leather and wood steering wheel, and moon roof.

"You got everything a new G-Wagen had plus what Brabus builders so graciously added to make this the only one on Earth."

He told her of the built in Sirius satellite radio and a built in police radar scanner and signal scrambler. Opening the rear of the G-Wagen, he showed her the JL Audio W7 twelve-inch woofers in custom-made fiberglass housing, painted to match the trunk and interior accents. It even came with leather and wood luggage and a champagne chiller in the center of the rear row. Javi spared no expense at all in having it built from the frame up, and unbeknownst to Michelle, certain life-saving technology and structuring had been added to keep her safe. Little did she know it, but Michelle now owned a V12 powered tank.

"Go around to the passenger's side, baby," Javi told her.

He followed her around and stood with her as she opened the door.

"I think there's something for you in the glove compartment," Javi then said.

Michelle noticed that everyone was eagerly watching, grins and smiles of anticipation on their faces. Nonetheless, she turned around and opened up the glove compartment. She gasped when she saw the little red box inside. Grabbing it, she turned back to face Javi. He had the biggest smile on his face as he took the box from her.

"Michelle, baby, you make me happier than anything in life ever could. I love you more than words can describe," Javi told her, gazing down into her eyes as she gazed back, her own eyes misting up. "Tu eres el amor de mi vida, y quiero estar contigo el resto de mi vida, amor. Can I have you forever?"

Michelle's tears of joy fell down her face.

"You've always had me, Papi, and you always will," she told him.

"Good."

He then sank to one knee before her and opened the box, revealing the custom-made, Harry Winston, eight-carat pink diamond set on a yellow-gold ring with baby pink diamonds around it.

"Marry me, baby. Be my…"

"Yes!" she suddenly screamed out, cutting him off. "I will! I'll be your wife! Yeeeesss!"

Everyone chuckled and laughed as they applauded. They watched Javi slide the twelve and a half million-dollar engagement ring onto his now fiancée's finger, then he stood. Michelle yanked him down by the collar of his shirts to kiss him.

"Ow!" Javi's chest wound pinged with pain as her move disturbed it.

"Oh, my God! I'm sorry!" Michelle panicked.

Javi chuckled.

"Pain is love, Mamita. And I love you more than I love drivin' trucks."

"Daaaaayuum, yo!" Macho shouted, standing next to his woman and G-Baby. "Yo, cuzzo don't love nothin' that much, Michelle! Homies!"

Yessy elbowed him as everyone laughed.

"The hell was that for?" he asked her.

She shrugged and smiled smugly as G-Baby giggled. Michelle got her a big kiss then. Javi tongued her down to the point that she felt like she was going to spontaneous combust. Her whole body yearned for him. He leaned in and spoke in a whisper next to her ear, his lips so close that Michelle felt them brush it.

"When I get you home tonight, amor, I'm putting another baby in you."

Michelle burst out laughing.

"I will let you try as many times as you want, mi handsome tiguere. If anybody can do some shit like that, it'll be you."

***

XAVIER

Later that night in Pittsburgh…

"Oooooo…. mmmm, Xavier… shit… goddamn, baby!" moaned Kenzie, lying on her back on the bed, ass naked with her red pumps still on. "Oh, my God, you are… sssss… ooooo fuuuuuck!"

She was in a whole other world at the moment. Her legs opened up wide, hands clenching the soft blanket, Xavier's face buried in her goodness gracious, devouring her. He went in on her, sucking her clit, drinking her sweet juices, while he used two fingers to stroke her tunnel. Minutes later, Kenzie exploded in his face, cumming so hard that her legs felt numb.

"Shit, Xavier! What the fuck did you just do to me?" Kenzie asked, having never climaxed that hard.

"I gave you that X-man lickity-split bang-bang!"

She burst out laughing as he stood, six feet three inches of dark toned muscular man with ten inches of dick, hard and ready for her.

"Mmmmm, my favorite!" Kenzie exclaimed, wrapping her hand around it and sliding forward to the edge of the bed.

"Your favorite, huh?" Xavier asked as Kenzie planted a kiss on the tip with her glossy red lips.

"Mmhmm." Kenzie opened her mouth and stuck her tongue out and smacked it with his dick. "Want me to show you?"

She then swirled her tongue around the head while she used her left hand to cup his balls and massage them.

"Yeessss," he groaned, loving how free she was with him.

Kenzie got to it. She opened wide and took him in deep. He went past the dangling thing at the back of her throat. Kenzie handled all of his cock like a pro while Xavier started thrusting in and out of her mouth.

"Fuck, girl! Goddamn!" Xavier cursed, throwing his head back, enjoying how good her mouth was.

She slid forward, getting on her knees. She used both hands to jerk his shaft while sucking, and it made Xavier go insane. He couldn't take it anymore. He pulled her up from the floor, tossed her onto the bed, and pounced on her. Kenzie laughed at his frenzied horniness then cried out in blissful ecstasy when she felt him enter her wet-wet.

"Xavier! Fuuck, baby, you feel so fuckin' good inside me!" she told him, wrapping her legs around his waist as he drove into her, pinning her wrists down on the bed, taking control.

"Tell me how good this dick is, baby," Xavier demanded, popping the shit out of the pussy now with power driving strokes.

"The best! Shit! It's the best I ever had!" Kenzie cried out.

"This my pussy?"

"Yes! You know it's yours!"

Xavier wiggled her loose from him then flipped her over onto her stomach. Kenzie tooted her ass up for him, staying face down, and bit on her lip as she felt him re-enter her from behind.

"I'm finna tear this phat, juicy ass the fuck up!" Xavier growled, as he went savage on her, jack hammering the pussy relentlessly while smacking her ass, pulling her hair, and talking dirty to her.

Kenzie reached her climax and again exploded so hard that she drenched Xavier. He knew what she liked last, to finish her off. Kenzie reached back, pulled her booty cheeks apart, and exposed her pink asshole.

"Put that thang up in this muthafucka, baby," Kenzie demanded of him.

Xavier spit a wad of saliva onto her puckered-up booty hole then rubbed his dick in it, getting it all lubed up. He eased in the tip, inching his way inside slowly, gently, careful not to hurt her.

"Mmmm, baby! Yeah! Fuck this ass, Xavier! Hit this shit!" she moaned out, squeezing the blanket in her hands, toes going wild in her pumps.

Xavier gave her a little more until she came once more. Then, as she felt his dick pulsating inside her anus, Kenzie knew he was close to cumming. He groaned gutturally – cursing, grunting, sweating his ass off. Kenzie muscled her way out of the doggy-style position, put him onto his back, and quickly hunched herself over him from the side; Kenzie started sucking his dick again, caring not at all that it'd just been up her asshole, until he busted his nut, filling her mouth with hot semen globs.

"Hooooly sheeeit!" Xavier shouted while Kenzie jerked and sucked him dry.

When she finished, she swallowed it all with a smile. Xavier laughed, pulling her to him, wrapping her up in his arms.

"You're amazing, Kenzie"

She giggled.

"You're wonderful, Xavier."

"We're dope," he then said and kissed her forehead.

She nodded her head in agreement.

"We most definitely are, baby," she agreed, tracing the line of his lips with her finger. "Thank you for coming into our lives."

Then, Kenzie's eyes closed, and she drifted off into a sex induce sleep. Xavier smiled to himself, then he said, "Thank y'all for comin into mines."

He closed his eyes then and floated off right behind her.

***

EVELYN

Smack!

"Ooww, bitch!" yelled Evelyn, fire in her eyes at Gloria, who had just smacked her bare ass, making her jump out of her sleep. "What the fuck?"

Oinky squealed in fear. He'd been sleeping on the pillow by Evie's head.

Gloria snapped back. "Because, bitch! You fucking moaning in yo sleep! Shut the tuck up!"

Evelyn had been dreaming of Prince. She only then realized that she had to have him. She looked up at Gloria, and suddenly, blinded with rage, she jumped up and charged her girlfriend like an angry bull. Evelyn swung calculated fists at Gloria, connecting the first three easily. Gloria yelped in pain from how hard her woman could hit. Oinky squealed even louder, as his humans fought, tearing into each other.

Gloria ducked the next two swings her girlfriend threw and countered with a hard right jab that made Evelyn's head snap upwards.

"¡Puta!" Evelyn screamed and rushed her, bum-rushing her. They both landed on the bed hard enough that Oinky was bounced off and hit the floor, squealing in pain.

"Oinky!"

Evelyn let go of Gloria and rushed to her piglet. He was more scared than actually hurt. She scooped him up into her arms and ran out of the bedroom naked to the bathroom.

Gloria was completely dumbfounded by her girlfriend's sudden blow up. She knew Evelyn was still stressing over her big brother but never had she displayed such rage toward her. Gloria could actually feel her jaw swelling up. She sat on the bed, not knowing what to do. The lights in their big, expansive, luxurious master bedroom were dimmed low. Music played at mid-volume. The sounds of Lil' Durks' *Like Me* featuring Jeremih crooned from the home audio system, wired around the earth-tone painted, hardwood floored bedroom. Gloria had been the one to design it and spent a bag on just the bedroom and plenty more on the rest of their 5,250 square foot home.

Sitting there, trying to think of a way to apologize without getting socked again, Gloria's peripheral view caught a light suddenly lighting up to her right. She looked and saw

Evelyn's iPhone vibrating. Never before had she gone through her woman's phone, but curiosity got to her in mere seconds. Gloria went over to the nightstand it set on and saw a text message from someone named Prince Handsome Chocolate. She went wide-eyed, then she saw the message.

I don't know what you did to me last night, but I can't stop thinking about you. Call me when you wake up, beautiful.

Gloria's hand came to her mouth, shocked to discover the message of infidelity. Her eyes welled up with tears as instant pains in her heart made her chest hurt. The phone's screen went black after a minute. Gloria then became furious. She heard Evelyn coming seconds later and moved away from the phone. Evelyn still had Oinky in her arms; the piglet snorted calmly now. Lying back on the bed, Evelyn said not a word and got under the Gucci blanket. Gloria stared at her for a minute, thinking in her head, *I will not lose you to no fucking Prince pussy-face! You are mine! ¡Por siempre!* She mentally swore then came up with a plan to make sure of that... forever.

Chapter 13

JAVI

The next morning, Javi was awakened by Michelle's phenomenal oral skills. Then, she slowly rode him, careful not to grab his chest like she was so used to doing. They went at it for a blissful half hour, then after a blazing hot quickie in the shower, they got dressed and went down to the kitchen where the dogs were waiting hungrily.

Michelle cooked scrambled cheese eggs with bacon. While she chefed it up, Javi went and invited Jamaica's goons inside for breakfast. Michelle made enough to feed all twenty of them, serving them first then Javi, Demon, Diamond, and herself last.

Javi called his sister after they ate to check on her.

"Hey, bro!" she answered, sounding excited.

"What's up, young lady? How're you doin' this mornin'?"

"I'm straight. On TruckPaper.com, getting more trucks and trailers. I went and picked Nena up. We over Kiki and Jada's crib right now. Payton and Olivia on the way; we probably finna go get our new trucks 'n shit today. How you?"

"I'm gucci. I'm happy to hear you on the biz. That's why Pop gave you that contract. Y'all deserve it. I didn't hear you say Gloria though. She ain't there?"

"No," Evelyn replied dryly.

Javi heard the tone in her voice.

"Somethin' happen?"

"I beat her ass."

"Again? Why now?"

"Because she slapped my ass while I was sleep and scared Oinky, bro!"

Javi tried so incredibly hard not to, but he just couldn't do it. He burst out laughing, which hurt his chest.

"It's not fuckin' funny, Javi! That shit hurt!"

Javi laughed and grimaced.

"I'm hangin' up, man."

"Naw, sis, chill. My bad."

Javi could hear Evelyn's girls laughing in the background.

"All y'all shut cha'll asses up or get the fuck out!" Evelyn shouted at them.

Javi listened as the twins went in on her ass. He put his phone on speaker, so Michelle could hear her bickering.

"Bitch, this is our house! How yo ass gon try ta throw us up outta hea'?" Jada asked.

"Yeah, with yo craz' ass," her twin added sassily.

"Because mirror-bitches! I'm Evie F Baby! ¡Yo hago lo que queiro, cabronas!"

"Oonga boonga 'ta yo ass too, wench," said Kiara.

"I'm bout to fire all y'all asses," Evelyn threatened. "Or… put y'all asses in automatic Freightliner Cascadia."

"I wish you would put me in an automatic, bitch," Olivia said. "I'll ride that punk ass shit into Lake Michigan and drown that ho!"

"Anyways, bro," Evelyn said as the ladies laughed. "When Xavier comin' back?"

"When Nena chills out," he told her.

He and Michelle both heard the sound of lips smacking.

"Yo ass can smack ya lips all you want, Nena," Michelle chimed in, "but if you really carryin' his seed, do you think the best way to make him want to be in your life is to fight chicks at truck stops?"

"She's fuckin' with my…"

135

"If you say your man, Azalia," Michelle interjected, cutting Nena off with her government name, "when you give birth, I'ma be the one throwin' them thangs at cha'. Xavier is not, and was never, your man. Y'all was fuckin' and were friends. Stop tryin' to force him to you 'cause you only pushin' him away."

She heard Nena smack her lips again.

"Aight, Michelle. He won't even talk to me though."

"That's cause you is a thirsty bitch." Michelle and Javi heard Evelyn clown.

"Okay. We out, yo," Michelle said then.

"Talk to y'all later, sis," Evelyn replied. "Love you both."

"Love you too."

"Byee, Michelle and Javi!" the other girls sang out.

"Deuces, crazy ladies," Javi told them and ended the call.

"Well, Evie has quite the crew, yo," said Michelle, getting up to clean up everything. "At least we know they crazy like her."

"Sheeeeeeeeeit! Ain't noooobody crazy like my sister."

"Not even ChaCha?" Michelle asked.

"Okay. Nobody but ChaCha."

"G-Baby?"

Javi twisted his lip.

"Okay, Gabriela too."

"And Yessinia?"

Javi narrowed his eyes at Michelle.

"Yessy is incomparable to any woman alive, bae," he told his fiancée. "She would make Griselda Blanco shit on herself out of fear."

Michelle laughed.

"I guess that's why they call her the Bad Rican."

***

XAVIER

Xavier opened the door to discover his grandparents there with smiles on their faces.

"Oh, snap! What are y'all doin' here?" Xavier asked.

"We came to meet this young lady and daughter that we hear you're shacking up with carriño," Maritza told him.

The creamy brown skinned woman looked like she could still pass for being in her late thirties or early forties instead of in her early sixties. Her hair was still solid brown, no dye to hide any grays. No wrinkles and barely a turkey neck. She stood five inches shorter than her massive, ox built six-foot-one husband, Diego, who was a little more caramel toned with a bald fade haircut, neat goatee, with grays by his temples. He didn't look sixty-five years old either but possibly a heavyweight wrestler in his forties.

Both of the ol' heads were dressed for a day of relaxation without any jewelry. The only indication that they were somebodies was from the brand-new Rolls-Royce Dawn convertible they'd hopped out of. And like Xavier, while in Pittsburgh, they rode without any Jamaican goons.

The Steel City and the rest of Pennsylvania was theirs. It was their home, but like any self-aware homeowner, there was still always security systems installed and trustworthy neighbors always ready to defend the block.

"I'm sure they'll both be happy to meet y'all," Xavier told them, stepping aside, so they could enter.

Precious heard the two O.G.s and came running down the stairs right up to them, greeting them with excited grunts and snorts, tail wagging a million miles an hour.

"Kenzie! Neveah! Somebody's here to meet you!" Xavier yelled up the stairs.

Seconds later, the two came down the stairs, dressed plainly for the day, Kenzie in a Pink t-shirt with a pair of leggings and flats, Neveah in a Pink velour hoodie outfit. Kenzie saw the two ol' heads there, both smiling at her and her daughter. Nevaeah saw them too, and to Kenzie's surprise, her little one was excited.

"Well, hello, pretty little girl!" Martiza gushed over Neveah, crouching down low to her eye level with Precious standing next to her. "What's your name?"

"Neveah Cardoza."

"Hi, Neveah! My name is Maritza Valdez! I'm Xavier's grandmother, and this is his grandfather, Diego! It is so nice to meet you!"

Diego reached out his hands and gave Kenzie a warm fatherly hug, embracing her. He'd already heard of what she had endured with the father of her daughter attacking her. The marks on her face were still there but had healed up for the most part.

Kenzie felt welcomed even more now. Maritza held her daughter, who giggled loudly. Thinking back on how she grew up in Zion, Kenzie realized she had never been accepted in anywhere because of her white skin, her height – which she'd grown tall in her teens – and she'd developed a voluptuous frame that so many other girls hated her for and tried to shame her. They called her a whore, fake, and she'd been the victim of all sorts of assaults. It was even worse because of her Crohn's disease. It flared up at so many of the wrong times, and she was teased so much for it that it was a wonder that she hadn't committed suicide.

When she met her daughter's father, he seemed to genuinely care about her. He treated her right, didn't see her as a slut or a piece of meat. When her Crohn's flared up one evening while they were stuck in heavy traffic on Chicago's Dan Ryan Expressway, he didn't boot her out of his car with a soiled bottom like others had done.

Then, when she got pregnant with Neveah, it all changed for the worse. He started beating her, shaming her, teasing her for her flare ups. Her hair was red because of him. She'd tried to change it up and be desirable for him again, but all it did was make him try to set her out for all his Vice Lord brothers to run trains on. That was when she had to go, and she did. She took her daughter, their things, and went to get her own apartment, supporting her young one and herself by working like an honest woman. Stacks wasn't willing to just let her go without harassing her.

"I am glad my grandson has two good ladies in his life," said Diego, as he released Kenzie. "He can finally stop jumping around."

"Como un charlatan," Maritza added, looking at Xavier, never having approved of him being a player but saying it in Spanish so as to not put him on blast in front of Kenzie.

Xavier chuckled.

"No soy un charlatan, abuelita."

"Uh huh. Suuure, papa," Maritza replied sarcastically. "That's why I am hearing that you are going to have a baby with Nena?"

Xavier sighed. "I hear the same thing."

Diego stayed quiet. News of Nena's pregnancy traveled fast, and Maritza had to know.

Kenzie spoke no Spanish, but she heard Nena's name and immediate grew tense. Neveah had no clue at all what was going on as she clung to Maritza, and Precious just sat there.

"Papa," the woman spoke to him again, "tu necisitas que ir hablar con ella muy pronto."

Xavier did not want to talk to Nena any time soon, but he knew that if he had a kid on the way, he had to be a man, and a man would not abandon his seed... ever!

***

Deciding to spend time together, Xavier was geeked for a day with the O.G.s The stories he'd heard of the notorious Diego and Maritza Valdez trumped any action movie. Xavier went and got dressed, putting on a crisp white t-shirt with Louis Vuitton on the chest in blue letters and blue LV monogrammed shorts with the custom blue and white LV low-top sneakers. He wore no jewelry, a little Versace cologne, then he brushed some Pink Lotion into his waves.

Ready to go, Xavier made sure Precious had plenty of food, water, and access to the basement where newspaper in a corner was laid down for her to use the bathroom.

Neveah wanted to ride with the ol' heads, so Xavier undid her car seat, took it out of the G-Wagen, and set it up in the rear row of the Rolls. He buckled her in, kissed her forehead, then Diego and Maritza got in. Xavier went and hopped up into the G-Wagen with Kenzie.

"Bae, can your grandparents see inside of here?" she asked him as Xavier push started the engine.

He put it in drive and started rolling.

"Can't nobody see inside, even wit' they faces pressed up against the windows."

"Good." Kenzie smiled mischievously and reached over to undo his shorts. "Cause I'm bout to suck the shit out of this dick while you drive this sexy ass truck."

She freed his hardness, got up on her knees, and lowered her head down into his lap with her mouth wide open. Xavier groaned, feeling her engulf him. He prepared himself to ride while she topped him off. Her skills were incredible and not a single one of his other ladies made him bust a nut so hard that he forgot his name like Kenzie did.

***

JAVI

At the new yard, Javi smiled as Michelle turned her new G65 Brabus truck in. Many of their trucks were gone as usual. The third garage bay door was up. Parked in front of it was Tool's glossy black Ford F-450 service truck and parked in the middle of the yard was his massive sparkling turquoise Kenworth T800 wrecker, chromed out with big exhaust pipes and gleaming wheels. It was a huge tow truck, much like the W900l he had that had gotten damaged during an ambush by hired hitters sent by Victor Gomez during the ride back to Illinois from Tool's oil refinery in Jersey, while

Javi, Xavier, Evelyn, and ChaCha were bringing back billions of dollars' worth of liquified cocaine in tanker trailers.

Javi saw that Tool and one of his skilled diesel mechanics that ran Tool's New Jersey glider kit truck business were there working on Nena's car hauler. The only rig in Xavier's heavy-haul division was his non-heavy-hauler Kenworth W900L. Javi knew Xavier was bringing on two more drivers to step his game up.

Inside the first bay, Javi's Pride and Class set in its spot. His dry van/intermodal crew was gone as well, out getting their money in new trucks Javi had gotten for them as well. Looking up at the barrier hanging over the office door, he saw Valdez Transport, LLC on it. Putting his thoughts together with his fiancée, the name dedicated had been put to rest, and the new company name had been born with Michelle as co-owner.

Michelle parked her SUV at the offices and killed the engine. As she opened her door to get out, she and Javi saw a clean, violent purple, drop Porsche 911 Turbo S entering the yard. Driving the sporty coupe was Valdez Transport's newest member of the team.

"Uh oh. Here comes the one that got away from bro," Javi said, seeing Xavier's childhood sweetheart behind the wheel.

Vanessa pulled up next to the G-Wagen and parked as Demon and Diamond got out of the rear. On the Persian-Rican's face was a cheerful smile that was as bright as the sun in the blue sky. She was dressed very boss like in a shiny leather Mugler dress that matched the Porsche. She had on glossy purple lipstick, black eyeliner, her hair pulled into a tight bun, gold Cartiers framing her gorgeous face, and down on her feet were cheetah print Red Bottom heels. Gold Cartier earnings dangled from her ears, flicking like the Cartier on her wrist.

Grabbing her purple diamond stitched Chanel bag from the rear seat of the 911, Vanessa walked around to Michelle and Javi, looking as happy as a pig in mud to be there.

"Heeeey!" sang Vanessa, hugging Michelle in a sisterly embrace. "I missed you so much, yo! Straight up, B."

"We missed you too, Ma. Last time I really got to see you, you ain't have all that booty behind you," Michelle said.

Javi burst out laughing.

"Shut up, Javier," Vanessa chuckled.

"My bad, but you was a twig, cuz."

She gave him the finger, then she started looking around. Michelle and Javi followed her eyes to see what she was looking for.

"You aight?" Javi asked.

"Mhmm. Yeah. Just... takin' it all in, you feel me? So, um, thanks for bringin' me in, you two. Feels good to get from under Ximena's thumb."

Michelle and Javi laughed.

"Ain't no thang. Go on and get ya space set up how you want it. We're about to head out," Michelle told her.

"Okay. Um, yeah... I'll do that," Vanessa said, looking around again. "Javi, it's good to see you up and at em, cuz. When that bitch gets caught, I would love to hit her in her shit a few times. You two drive safely, and I'll be here if you need me."

Vanessa patted Demon's then Diamond's heads before she sauntered off, entering the building.

"She been lookin' for Xavier. You know that, right?" Michelle said to Javi.

"She been lookin' for that nigga since she came to Illinois," Javi replied. "I'm just not sure I wanna be around when she finds him with a girl that has a kid and a pregnant side piece."

"Ooooooweee... that sounds like a crazy chick flick movie, yo," Michelle said, shaking her head.

Chapter 14

Javi pre-tripped his Pride and Class then pulled it out of the garage. Michelle and the dogs climbed up inside, then Javi rolled over to where a few of his trailers were. He backed up to one of his forty-eight-foot long flatbed trailers, got hooked up, then pulled off with the trailer rolling behind him. Nena entered the yard in her Chevy as he approached the exit. She waved out her window at him. He tooted his horn at her, then reaching the road, he made a wide left turn to head into Wisconsin.

Lil' Scrappy's *Be Real* featuring Trillville bumped from the stock audio system. Javi hated riding without pavement pounding bass. He couldn't wait until Tool could get his new truck into one of his shops. Tool's rapidly growing glider kit truck building business was combined with his big diesel power repair business. With him, Tool had a team of crafty ASE certified diesel techs and custom fabricators that took used and new trucks – and even buses – and turned them into show quality vehicles. His business built some of the best gliders in the country. Wealthy company owners and well-off drivers flocked to him for custom builds or to drop a bag on a build which never cost less than $125,000.

***

Leaning back in her seat, Michelle stroked behind Demon's ears as Sevyn Streeter's *It Won't Stop* featuring

Chris Brown came on. She glanced over at her man and couldn't help but to admire him. To her, he was all that and a bag of chips. Just a few days ago, she had found him laid out on the floor of a restaurant with a knife in his chest, bleeding out. Now, he was behind the wheel of a new, nearly four hundred thousand dollar truck that she had gotten him to buy, a ridiculously expensive diamond engagement ring was on her finger, and she had a Mercedes G-Wagen that was the only one in the entire world.

Then, she thought about the baby in her belly that they had created out of the purest love. It had her so happy that she almost cried. Soon, Michelle planned to get started on creating her custom diamond and fine jewelry line. She wanted to give Tiffany & Co, Cartier, and Jacob & Co a run for their money with all of her designs.

***

EVELYN

"Oh, shit! Yo, that was her!" shouted Evelyn when she saw the bright red SRT8 Jeep Cherokee shoot past her in the westbound land of 21st Street in Zion.

In the car with her was Payton, Olivia, Kiara, and Jada. They were thrown to their right when Evelyn slammed down on the brake pedal and yanked her wheel to the left, hitting a 180-degree spin in the middle of the street.

"Goddamn, Eve! Who is you talkin' about?" asked Payton, rubbing her shoulder as Evelyn hit the gas and took off in pursuit of the Jeep.

"That's the bitch that stabbed my brother!" Evelyn told them as her engine roared.

"Oh, heeeell no! Catch that bitch, Eve!" Olivia shouted from the rear, pulling out a Glock .40 from her handbag and cocking it.

The twins pulled out twin Sig Sauer .40 calibers. Payton got her Taurus .40 out. Evelyn grabbed her bag and got her

Desert Eagle .40 out, keeping her eyes focused on the rear of the Jeep as she sped her ass off coming back upon Zion-Benton High School. As fast as she could, Evelyn made a call to her big cousin. He answered in three rings.

"¿Qué lo qué, lil cuz?" Macho said.

"Cuz! Pleeaase tell me you're in Zion!"

"I am bout to leave my crib. Why you yellin'?"

Evelyn told him who she had her eyes on as they spoke.

"Bet. Bring that bitch my way. I'll take it from there," Macho told her.

Evelyn ended the call and got ready. She had no intentions of letting the bitch live ten minutes past when the first bullet was fired from her cannon.

***

Packed up and ready to get the hell out of the danger zone after stabbing a very respected and loved man in her restaurant and leaving him for dead, she knew her time was limited if she didn't flee. He had a lot of family and friends, and not a single one of them hesitated to get wild wherever they were.

Enroute to Mitchell International Airport in Milwaukee, Angela already had things set up for her in Caye. It had been a long time since she had been back to Puerto Rico. She had left broke, starving, sucking and fucking to survive. She was going back with plenty of money and a reason beyond herself to live.

Nodding her head to a song by Wisin y Yandel, Angela's attention went to the sounds of tires screeching. She peeped the big silver BMW that had passed by her a second ago slam on its brakes then whip back around, about facing. It disappeared behind the three vehicles that were trailing behind her as she passed the high school approaching Kenosha Road.

Thinking nothing of it, her mind went to Javi and how he had shitted on her, treating her like she was just some bitch he was fucking instead of a woman that had a heart and feelings. She was Puerto Rican. It wasn't in her to allow a man to get down on her, and then he had come to the restaurant to physically harm her. So, she got him first, catching him off guard and driving a steak knife into his chest; then, she immediately freaked out when she realized what she had just done. She took off running, hightailing it out of the restaurant that he bought for her, hiding in one of the stores in the plaza her spot was in until she felt she could go get the SRT8 Jeep that he bought her and get ghost.

Angela came to the stop sign at 21st and Kenosha Road. She had just come to a complete stop sign when the same BMW that had hit a 180 spin a little while back screeched to a stop right next to her, blocking the oncoming lane.

"¿Qué carajo?" Angela said to herself, looking over at it.

Both of the darkly tinted front and rear passenger windows rolled down then. Angela screamed when she not only saw three guns pointed at her but also when she locked eyes with Javi's crazy baby sister.

"¡Cono!" Angela screamed and mashed the gas as shots were fired at her.

The windows on her side exploded as they kept coming. Angela kept the gas pedal to the floor. The BMW was right on her ass as if she was in a Toyota Camry and not a Jeep with a supercharged Hemi engine under the hood. Bullets took out the rear window of her SUV. A few hit her dashboard; she screamed in agony when one hit her in the back of her right shoulder.

Angela cried her eyes out as the white-hot searing pain nearly made her faint. She couldn't give up though. Life wasn't just her now. She had to live for the both of them. As more shots came, Angela reached Green Bay Road. She hit a hard right and aimed for Route 173. The Beamer was still on her. It got on her rear and nearly pushed her toward Green

Bay and 173, but no more shots were fired. Angela glanced in her rearview and was just able to see the face and golden hair of her ex-lover's baby sister.

"¡Dios mio!" Angela cried, truly realizing that the devil in Dominican form was on her heels and would not stop until she was dead.

Angela risked it all as the light at 173 turned red. She shot right through the intersection seconds before east and westbound traffic started crossing through. Tires screeching behind her made her look in the mirror again in time to see the BMW had been blocked.

"Yes! Yes! Fuck you, bitch!" Angela screamed out, coming upon a subdivision to her right. "I cannot be caught! Jodete, y tu hermano!"

Angela kept glancing in her rearview, hoping to create a major gap before the BMW got back in pursuit. She was so busy looking back that she didn't notice the eighteen-wheeler pull out of the subdivision, stretching across the two-way road, blocking it off completely, until she was about ten seconds or so from it.

"¡Coño!" she screamed, slamming on her brakes.

Her SUV skidded out of control, sliding sideways. Angela cried out in pure fear as she slammed into the driver's side of the semi at nearly fifty miles an hour. She hit with such impact that her SUV nearly split into two pieces. She was hurled into the passenger's seat upon impact, face smacking against the door hard, breaking her nose and fracturing her jaw while a gaping wound opened up on her forehead.

Broke up and in agonizing pain, Angela couldn't move. She whimpered, shattered pieces of glass in her skin hurting her so bad. Her shot shoulder still bled profusely. She started fading in and out when, just then, her crumpled driver's door was yanked open, and a strong pair of hands snatched her out of the destroyed car. Angela saw a very muscular man with braids and colored eyes wearing a black tank top that let those bulky tattooed arms and chest show. He had fire in his eyes like a demon. A caramel-colored woman appeared then and walked up to Angela. With strength she didn't even look like she had, she snatched Angela up off the ground.

"¡Aaayyy!" she screamed in pain from all over her body.

The girl pulled out a Glock and put it to Angela's jaw just as the BMW skidded to a stop just feet away.

"¡Estas muerto, puta!" the caramel girl growled through clenched teeth.

"No, let me do it!"

Angela saw Javi's sister running toward her with a huge handgun in her hand.

"No! No! ¡No me mates! Please!"

She wondered why no other people driving along had come yet or called the cops. She didn't even hear sirens. Caramel flung her on the ground and aimed her pistol at her, and so did Evelyn and the four other girls that had hopped out of the Beemer.

***

EVELYN

"There is no mercy, mamahuevo!" growled the gold-haired Dominican girl, pointing her big .40 at her. "You tried to kill my brother! Now you die!"

"¡Estoy embarazada!" Angela shouted then.

Javi's sister and the bulky, braided up trucker thug both went wide eyed. The four other girls had no clue what was said. Evelyn clenched her teeth as tears filled her eyes.

Angela cried out again. "Please no kill me, Evelyn! I'm pregnant! It is Javier's child!"

"¡Mentirosa!" Evelyn screamed, "Liar!" at her and wrapped her finger around the trigger.

But just as she was about to put the whole remainder of her clip into Angela's face, her big cousin laid a hand on the gun, forcing her to hold off.

"Macho!" Evelyn cried. "¡Esa outa trató matar a mi hermano!"

"I know, Eve, that she tried to kill ya brother. But if she's pregnant for real, you'd be murderin' ya own niece or nephew."

"So, what! We just let her go?"

"No," interjected Yessinia as she tucked her Glock back into her waistline. "We take this bitch and hold her for Javi. Whatever he wants done will happen."

Angela swallowed hard then. The next thing she knew, another woman that she hadn't seen came out of nowhere and kicked her so hard in the face that it knocked Angela unconscious.

***

XAVIER

Over in Pittsburgh's Homestead business district area, Xavier, Kenzie, Neveah, and the ol' heads were having a ball at the famous Dave & Buster's arcade which set just minutes away from the famed water park, Sand Castle, and only a ten-minute drive away was Pittsburgh's historic theme park, Kennywood.

Neveah had never been to such a place before. She felt like she had been taken to a magical world of games and prizes. Kenzie knew about Dave & Buster's but had never been inside one herself. All she knew was that people said they were dope and at night became a bar.

Xavier had been to the arcade spot plenty of times, but this time in particular, he was having the best time ever. Kenzie and Neveah brought him so much joy. He felt like it was destiny for him to have met them. To him, it looked like the only time Kenzie had been this happy was possibly when Neveah was born, and with how Kenzie's baby daddy had been since the little girl was born, Xavier doubted that the four-year-old had ever had this much fun.

Even Diego and Maritza were having a blast until a phone call seemed to change their moods a little. Xavier had asked them what was up. They both told him everything was fine. He didn't believe them, but he knew if it was something big, he'd eventually find out.

For the majority of the day, they enjoyed playing games and bonding. Kenzie quickly developed a strong bond with Xavier's grandparents as Neveah did. By the end of their evening at the arcade, Neveah was tuckered out. Xavier and Kenzie had planned to do a little more, but since the toddler was ready for bed, they'd have to save it for another day.

"Nonsense," said Diego. "We can keep la princesa with us, so you two can go enjoy yourselves. Kenzie deserves a nice night out, Papa."

"Sí, cariño," agreed Maritza. "Take your beautiful lady for a night out. We can go to your house and spend time with Neveah and Precious."

Xavier looked at Kenzie. "You okay with that?"

Her daughter was sitting on her lap, head resting against Kenzie's chest, already asleep. Kenzie smiled at her then looking at Xavier, she nodded her head.

"I'm down. My baby gets tired so easily."

"We'll take care of her, Kenzie," Maritza swore as she and her husband stood up, ready to go.

Kenzie stood up and handed the sleeping little one to Maritza. She kissed Neveah's cheek, then Xavier kissed her cheek, his grandmother's, and embraced his grandfather.

"Your papa and mother will see you all soon," Diego said to him.

"Word!" Xavier said with excitement.

"Yes. Talk soon, Papa, okay? Enjoy the night."

Diego and Maritza left with Neveah. Xavier took Kenzie's hands into his and pulled her up and wrapped his arms around her. Kenzie smiled up at him but found herself feeling shy all of a sudden. It was really the first time since they had met that they would actually be alone, and it had her excited as hell.

"So, what chu' tryna do, gorgeous? The sky is not the limit."

Kenzie giggled, wrapping her arms up around his neck.

"I want to have the greatest time ever with you. I don't care what that consists of as long as I'm with you, babe."

She pulled him down and kissed him passionately. His hand trailed down her sides to her ass and cupped it. Their kiss heated up as they blocked the other people out and disappeared in each other's embrace.

"Maaaan, if you kiss me like that again, I'ma have to buy my mans a new G-Wagen cause me 'n you gon' have it smellin' like sex permanently."

Kenzie burst out laughing at him, then she grabbed the collar of his shirt again.

"I have an idea of what we can do, babe," she told him, then she whispered to him.

Xavier lit up like a Christmas tree.

"Bet! Let's go!" he eagerly replied then took her hand and pulled her out of there so fast that her shadow nearly had to run to catch up.

Chapter 15

JAVI

After shooting up Mount Horeb, Wisconsin and picking up a load of rebuilt truck engines, transmissions, and other truck parts then delivering them to a train yard by the Dells, Javi shot south to pick up a load of new septic tanks in Beloit that he delivered to Oshkosh. His last run was to Pleasant Prairie where he picked up two boom lift machines that were going right to Racine.

***

Javi down-shifted gears with the jake on, coming to a stop light at 104th in Pleasant Prairie's big factory filled section. Michelle rubbed Demon's ears while his mate leaned against Javi. A few Escalades with the armed Rastas were right behind him. Kevin Gates' *Really Really* blared from the speakers, continuously making Javi wish for some bass.

As he and his fiancée sat at the red light, a prehistoric looking Peterbilt heading west on 104th, rolling slowly, pulling a lowboy trailer loaded with a medium sized Caterpillar excavator, gave both Javi and Michelle the creeps. It was black, faded; its stainless-steel exterior parts, wheels, its tall, and pointed exhaust pipes had no shine. It reminded them of those old Petes cast in movies where crazy, psychotic truck drivers ran people off of the road, then snatched them up, and they were never seen again.

Michelle caught the chills at the very sight of it, let alone how its roaring engine sounded like an angry T-Rex to his CB as the old 359 extended hood pulled all the way through the intersection.

"Aye, there, how bout cha drive? Don't that creepy ol Peterbilt belong in a scrap yard instead of spookin' up these here roads?" Javi asked, speaking like a redneck country boy.

A second later, the light turned green, and the driver's voice crackled through the C8.

"That almost sounded like my lil hatin' ass cousin, but ain't no way he in that pretty ass Pete I just passed by in my monster."

Javi started making a left turn, getting ready to reply, when Michelle came and hopped on his lap, taking the mic from him.

"¡Oye, tigueraso! ¡Que pasooooo, primo!" she hollered excitedly to the driver as Javi completed his turn.

"Whaz hannin', killa?! Ya mans dun finally seen the bright light that is a Peterbilt, huh?"

Javi chuckled as he shifted gears, going up a curved upgrade, trying to catch up with his cousin, who had already created a very wide gap between them with his wickedly fast ol' school.

"Thanks to me, yes, he has, yo. Where you on the way to though?" she asked as Javi reached the last gear on the low range of his transmission and buttoned up to the high range side, going to low sixth.

"Up to Caledonia to drop this lil Kitty Cat off. Y'all?"

"Sturtevant. Yo, where's Yessy and Gabi at?"

"Ion know, "he replied, then Michelle and Javi heard him laughing.

"Okay, butt head," Michelle called him as Javi passed by the big Red Plex center, gunning it on the straight away with his cousin's taillights in sight.

"Tell him to meet us at the Skillet when he drops the excavator," Javi told her, fast approaching the big shopping district that set along I-94 and Route 60.

Michelle relayed the message. Javi saw his cousin had come to a stop at a red light across from a big BP gas station. He got into the left lane to pull up next to the ol' school Pete. He crept up slowly, coming alongside the rear of the three axle lowboy trailer, passing by the backwards facing dirt digging machine.

Javi hit the button to the passenger window, rolling it down as he came up alongside the 1985 359 extended hood Peterbilt. He and Michelle could both hear and feel the powerful bass of Gucci Mane's *Stoopid* as it pounded from the classic rig.

Demon jumped up onto the passenger's seat as Javi came to a stop. Diamond went in front of the seat and stood on her hind legs to see out of the window with her mate. The tinted window of the ol' school Pete rolled down just then. Behind the wheel, the braided up, blue-gray eyed, Steel City Mafia goon sat with a grin on his face.

"Well, would'ja look at the lovebirds and their pups," Macho said with a chuckle.

Javi and Michelle heard barking coming from the inside of Macho's truck.

"Yo, cuz, yo ass got El Viejo out," Javi hollered out, calling Macho's Pete by the nickname he and his brother had dubbed the creepy ass truck since they rebuilt it. "And the dogs? You must be on a mission."

Macho shook his head.

"Naw, my legacy got hit by a dumb bitch. Gotta get her in the shop, so El Viejo had to wake up 'n make me some money, yah mean, lil cutty?"

"Oh, snap," Javi said, knowing that Macho was zealot when it came to his customized Legacy Class edition Peterbilt, mainly because it had been used to fulfill the last good weeks of his and his brother's mother's life before cancer took her away from them. "How bad did you beat the bitch that did it?" he asked right as the light turned green for them.

Macho chuckled. "I didn't touch her, lil cuz. I'ma leave it to you to handle the bitch, yo," he said then reared off, leaving Javi and Michelle with puzzled looks on their faces while flames shot up out of his truck's exhaust stacks.

***

EVELYN

She was still fuming about Macho refusing to let her blow Angela's head off. She cruised silently in her BMW. The only sound was Twista and The Speedknot Mobstaz's *Dreams* playing from her sound system.

Enroute to Joliet to a truck dealership, Evelyn had her ladies in Alpina with her. Payton, Olivia, Kiara, and Jada shared Evelyn's fury, wishing that they could have been the ones to avenge Javi. They at least hoped that they got to see him chop the bitch's head off.

***

Gloria had been calling and texting Evelyn non-stop until Evelyn cut her phone all the way off. Before she did though, she sent a text to certain people that she was sure would help her keep her eyes on the bright future and not on negativity. When she finally arrived at the dealership with her dread head goon squad in two Hummers, Evelyn found the dealerships' sales manager with an attitude for the delay in her scheduled pick-up time.

The Rastas made him bite his tongue when they hopped out of their SUVs, strapped up and wearing Kevlar. Evelyn pulled out her wallet, which looked like a Bible, and peeled off a few honchos to shut him up.

Parked in a row, ready for them, were four brand new Peterbilt 389 car haulers, all of them able to carry up to ten vehicles. They were all two-tone colors and had luxurious leather and wood grain interiors with comfortable sleeper berths.

With her new contract soon to kick off, Evelyn needed more trucks and more reliable drivers. Her girls that had been down with her since she joined her brothers were ready to ride for Evelyn until the wheels fell off.

While they went to get the keys, plates, and paperwork for their trucks, Evelyn was escorted to where her new truck – that wasn't new – awaited her. She was brought to a huge 2006 Volvo 880 with metallic burnt-orange paint and a sleeper berth that was so big that Shaquille O'Neal could jump inside of it and not hit his head on the ceiling. Evelyn had always wanted an 880.

It had a big 660 horsepower Cummings engine, a 13-speed transmission, air ride suspensions, and a deluxe interior. It was going to make the $78,000 her brother paid for it back in less than six months. It was rebuilt and essentially a new rig, ready to make money.

Gloria and Nena had new trucks as well, but theirs were at another dealership, and Evelyn was beyond grateful that Tool had volunteered to go with them to pick theirs up, and from another dealership, a few of the Jamaican goons had used a few of ChaCha's PJ&D Transport trucks to go pick up a few more luxury car-carriers for Evelyn's fleet.

With the trucks she already had and nine new ones, Evelyn had plans to make a huge name for Valdez Transport's Exotic Auto Transport division, all the while making her mother, father, brothers, and their grandparents proud of her. With sixteen trucks working, bringing in a few grand each daily for domestic transport, double for exotic and foreign, Evelyn and her girls would be seeing comma after comma after comma.

As Evelyn looked over her big 880, she noticed a clean, black. big body Audi A8 enter the dealership on chromed rims, tinted out all the way around. Her iPhone started ringing as it came to a stop by her BMW. She pulled it out of her back pocket and saw it was him calling.

"Hey, you," she answered, unable to hold back her smile.

"What up, gorgeous? Is that you over there by the orange truck?" Prince asked her.

"Yes indeed, handsome. I'm almost ready to go. Come on over," she told him.

The Audi rolled over. The three Rastas that were with her pulled their thumpers out and were about to pop at it until Evelyn told them it was a friend of hers inside. They relaxed but kept their eyes on the A8 as it pulled up.

Evelyn's smile grew tenfold when her tall, dark, and handsome new toy got out from behind the wheel, wearing a tank top that let his tattooed upper body flex, designer jeans, and sneakers with a fresh haircut and diamond jewelry around his wrist, neck, and in his ears.

"Well, damn!" he said, looking at the dread heads. "Fellas, I come to Eve in peace. Please do not shoot."

Evelyn chuckled as he walked past them and went to her, pulling her into his arms and kissing her. She instantly started getting weak in the knees, but right then, she realized what she was doing in front of everyone that knew she was in a relationship. Evelyn jumped back with wide eyes, a hand over her mouth, shocked at herself for so easily getting wrapped up in Prince.

"Uh oh… did I do something wrong?" he asked with a smile that said he didn't really care as long as he got some more of her soon.

"Um." Evelyn glanced past the Rastas to where her girls were. She sighed in relief when she saw they weren't paying any attention. "No… but… um… just, uh, hop in my car and follow me," she told him, aroused and nervous at the same time.

"Aight, love. Let's roll,' he agreed then headed to her Alpina.

Evelyn looked at the Audi he had pulled in and was about to ask why he was leaving his car behind when it suddenly pulled off, tires screeching as whoever was behind the wheel mashed the gas pedal.

"The hell?" she said to herself with a raised eyebrow as the Audi dipped out of the dealership like it was racing against time.

***

Seven Minutes Prior…

Man, what the fuck?! On Vice Lord! That's that bitch from the Burger King! Cuzzo fuckin wit' her!

He looked at his older cousin walk right up to the thick chick that had been looking around the engine bay of a big orange semi before he pulled up and almost got them blasted by some old dread heads.

He watched the girl look like her legs were going to give out as his cousin tongue kissed her, then she suddenly jumped away from him, looking around like she was scared of her boyfriend catching her. A minute later, he saw Prince walk off, heading toward a big body BMW. Looking back at the windshield, he saw the chick staring in his direction, but he knew for a fact that she couldn't see him.

He jumped over to get behind the wheel then.

Big cuz, you just solved my biggest dilemma, my nigga. I'm bout to get back, and yo bitch and who I know her people are finna regret playin' with a real ghost like me, joe. Five, he thought to himself.

He slammed it in drive, hit the gas, and whipped his cousin's Audi around, glancing at the girl in the rearview mirror, seeing that she was still watching as were the dread heads.

"Yeah, keep watchin', bitch. I'm on yo' ass. You and yo' people bout to pay for how y'all got down on me and my nigga, Rambo."

Chapter 16

KENZIE

"Ooooooo! Fuck, baby! Yees! That feel so goood!" she moaned, feeling all of Xavier inside of her while she leaned over, gripping the safety rail with her little skirt up and her thong to the side.

Up on one of the big viewing pads of the Overlook, Xavier was busy fulfilling Kenzie's request for him to give it to her raw and hot up on the top of the world. He gripped her hips and stuffed her wetness, giving her divine pleasure with downtown Pittsburgh across the river.

"Tell me how it feels, baby," Xavier grunted as he kept on stroking her. "I wanna hear it again."

"Like H-Heaven, Xavier! It feels l-l-like... oooo! Like Heaven, baby!"

She felt her orgasm building. Xavier could feel her clenching around him. Her body shook and trembled. She was about to cum all over him. Seconds later, she exploded all over his dick and his thighs. Her climax set his off. He busted his nut right after hers, cumming inside of her, too weak with his bliss to pull up out of the pussy.

"¡Coño, Mami!" Xavier exclaimed, panting with his dick still inside of her.

Kensie started laughing then.

"Oh, my God, Xavier! I can't believe we just did that!"

"Why?" he asked, pulling out of her, pulling his boxer briefs and shorts up while Kenzie fixed her thong and her skirt. "You said you wanted to get dicked down up on top of the world, baby."

"Yeah, but I didn't know there will be people out here too!"

Xavier looked at the viewing pads to the left and to the right. Both had people huddled up on them, all of them either looking at him and Kenzie with shock or snickering at how they had just got it in without a care in the world that they were in public, across the street from where people actually lived.

"Fuck them. What they gon' do? Nothin'," he replied. "All that matters is you and me."

"Aww! Bae, you are too damn good to be truuuueee! Where have you been all my life?" she asked, putting her arms around him.

"Lookin' for a good woman like you," he replied. "The night is young though. There's still places to see. I been wantin' to show you where me, my bro, and my sister came up at when we lived out this way with our cousins."

"Bet. Let's go see your childhood house then, handsome. I wanna see what contributed to you bein' the man that you are."

"Alrighty then, gorgeous," Xavier agreed, giving her ass a squeeze. "Let's get outta here and take a trip to the most live hood in Pittsburgh, Pennsylvania."

***

JAVI

Javi delivered the boom lifts to a military base in Sturtevant. He got his paperwork signed to confirm delivery for the factoring company he used to get paid after each load delivered by his trucks, minus the small percentage they got for shooting the delivery fee into his business account right away instead of him having to wait thirty days or more for the owners of the loads to issue payments.

While he handled the business with the military gate sergeant, Michelle got Demon and Diamond out on their leashes and walked them, so they could get some air, stretch their legs, and use the bathroom. Once done, they all got back into the Pride and Class, and Javi made his way to the Skillet to meet up with his cousin.

Arriving at the truck parking section minutes after leaving the Army base, Javi entered the lit-up lot and maneuvered his rig amongst the parked trucks, finding a spot in the rear with I-94 behind him. He backed into the spot and parked. He put his E-log onto 'Off Duty', then he cut his engine off.

Michelle kissed her dogs' noses, then she and Javi prepared to get out of the Pete. Before either of their feet touched the ground, they both heard the deafening roar of El Viejo's jake brake. They saw the ol' school riding along the side road of the truck lot, heading toward the entrance, no longer loaded with the excavator.

It made a wide turn in, rolled around the center island of parked trucks, and crept up the path toward where Javi and his fiancée were posted in front of his truck with the dread heads posted by their vehicles across from them.

Macho rolled along slowly, passing them. They saw the big head of his woman's German rottweiler hanging out of the passenger window. He pulled all the way past them, cutting a left turn and bringing his rig to a stop. He shifted into reverse and backed in next to Javi's truck, making his own spot that wasn't actually there.

When Macho killed the ferocious engine, it sounded like an angry lion being put back into its cage, but not without a fight. Javi and Michelle walked over to the driver's door as Macho opened it up. At his side, they saw that he had not only Maliante with him but Dreams as well, his female, tiger-brindle, old family, red nose pit bull, a little beast with chipped ears and green eyes that was of champion bloodlines. Demon and Diamond barked out of the Pride and Class at Dreams and Maliante, communicating with their furry friends.

Macho climbed out of his ol' school rocking a black Dickie suit with his nickname on the chest patch, a white-gold Cuban link chain around his neck, with a blacked-out Cartier on his wrist. On his feet were rare black and 'Yelphant-print Air Yeezy 1s. His braids were frizzy, but his beard and baby hair were freshly lined.

He dapped Javi up then hugged Michelle, but then from out of the opened driver's door came the Nuyorican who had been in the box-shaped sleeper the whole time. Yessy was clad in a tight t-shirt with spike toed Christian Louboutin pumps decaled across her chest, a pair of leggings, and on her feet, the spike toed Red Bottoms displayed on the chest of her shirt. She rocked her long silky hair down and had a New York snapback on her head, giving her that sexy thug misses that she epitomized so well. Then, right behind Yessy, came G-Baby, rocking a skin-tight, shoulder-less bodysuit with stilettos on her feet and her hair wet from the mousse she had styled it with. No matter what, Javi and Michelle were always amazed by Macho and the beautiful Puerto Rican gangstresses. They were, by definition, dope!

Michelle looked up at the 6'3" tall Dominican.

"Asshole," she called him for lying to her about where Yessy and G-Baby were, then she turned to the Nuyorican and the gangsta boo, as G-Baby was often called.

"What's goodie, yo? Why y'all let this nigga lie like that?"

Yessy chuckled as she hugged the much shorter than her Michelle.

"Don't trip. I smacked his ass while he was unchainin' that excavator, yo."

"I did too," said G-Baby in a feminine, raspy, Keyshia Cole like voice.

"Anyways," Macho interrupted. "I am famished. Instead of jaw-jackin' out here, how bout we go in there?" He pointed at the restaurant. "So, I can get me one of them fire ass sausage, egg, biscuit 'n gravy platters."

"Sounds *sooo* motherfucking *flame* right now! Let's go!" Javi said, taking his woman's hand to pull her along.

Yessy jumped up on Macho's back and made him giddy up. He took off with her on his back, leaving them all in the dust. G-Baby walked with Javi and Michelle, looking at her two best friends. Javi and Michelle both noticed the look on G-Baby's face.

"If you say it, I will slap you," Michelle managed to whisper to Javi without G-Baby hearing her.

Javi snickered to himself but didn't utter a word, knowing his feisty future wife would definitely do it.

***

Hmmm…

Sitting behind the wheel of a stolen Dodge Ram, the devil watched the five chop it up for a second at the front of the scary looking truck that had parked next to one that looked brand new. He saw the SUVs parked across from where his mark had backed the shiny new truck in and hadn't seen them get out until after the big guy with braids ran off with a thick ass chick on his back, then his primary green eyed target, holding the hand of his woman, headed toward the trucker restaurant with another chick at their side.

One, two… I'm coming for you… three, four… fuck you and your whore… five, six… I'm sick of you, bitch… seven, eight… I've sealed your fate… pinche prieto, he thought to himself, then he started laughing at himself, starting his engine and putting it in drive.

***

MICHELLE

In the dining section, Michelle stood with Yessy and G-Baby while Macho and Javi had waiters put together a big table to accommodate the five of them, Bullet and his crew, plus three more after Macho and Javi were notified by Tool that he was enroute with Gloria and Nena and some dreads.

While she chopped it up with the ladies, Michelle noticed a dark colored pickup truck creeping along outside. She couldn't see who was inside, but with its driver side window rolled down, she could see the silhouette of a man with long hair. Yessy saw Michelle's eyes were locked onto something. Both she and G-Baby followed where her eyes were and saw the pickup stop right outside.

Macho happened to see the ladies staring out of the window. He looked and saw the pickup. The flame for the lighter sparked as the driver lit a cigarette. On instinct, Macho, without a word, started walking toward the restaurant's exit, leaving Javi with a puzzled look on his face.

"Where's he going?" he asked the girls right as Yessy and G-Baby stepped out of their heels and hurried to follow.

The dreads then hurried to catch up as well. Javi turned to his woman and saw her looking out of the window. He looked and saw the pickup, then he saw his cousin quick stepping toward it. When Javi saw Macho start running at it, he cursed himself, stepping in front of his pregnant fiancée instinctively, shielding her from any bullets he anticipated flying through the window at any moment.

***

MACHO

He shot off like he had been flung form a sling shot, running full speed toward the pickup. The driver flicked the cigarette out and mashed the gas, taking off from where he had been watching them.

"¡Te veo pronto, puto!" Macho heard the driver shout as he sped off, laughing loudly.

Macho was about to up the FN he had in his waistline and start dumping until Yessy reached his side and stopped him.

"Not here, baby. Too many people," she reminded him.

"Dodge Ram pickup! Heading your way! Get that muddafucka!" He heard Bullet shouting.

G-Baby, Yessy, and Macho turned in time to see him yelling into his phone, getting word to the few of his goons that were still in the parking lot. The Ram was long gone already though. Javi stepped out of the restaurant with his pistol in his hand, trying to keep Michelle inside but failing miserably at it. She pushed her way out with a pistol in her hand as well, looking for the pickup.

People in the restaurant panicked as the mob grew deeper and deeper out front. Anticipating a shootout, they all ducked and waited for the bullets to fly. Macho pulled his phone from his pocket and made a call. It was answered almost immediately.

"¿Dimelo que paso, papito?" answered his great aunt, Maritza.

"I'm really tired of not bein' able to have a calm day, Tia. I think it's time we bring this thing with Mr. Gomes to an end."

"Diga no mas, Antonio," she replied, then the call ended.

He looked at his woman and G-Baby.

"This ends now. Let's go, yo," he demanded, walking back toward his cousin.

"To where?' the barefoot Nuyorican asked with her barefoot homegirl right with her.

"To ChaCha's make a bitch nigga cry chamber," he told them then hollered for Javi and Michelle to follow them back to Illinois.

Chapter 17

XAVIER

After heading back to his crib so he and Kenzie could get showered and fresh to hit the hood, seeing that Diego and Maritza were chillaxing on the couch in the living room with Precious laid out at their feet as they watched a classic movie and Neveah asleep up in the bedroom, Xavier and Kenzie headed right back out to the G-Wagen and left, heading toward Homewood to turn up.

At the corner of Brushton and Kelly, the tall, brick building had a line of scantily clad women and men rocking designer, some rocking real diamond jewelry, while others faked the funk. A hit song from Pittsburgh Street rapper Hardo blared, and people turned up outside as they waited to get into The Steel City Club.

Xavier parked the G-Wagen right in front at the entrance door and hopped out in a white and blue Gucci jean and jacket fit with blue Tims on his feet, dripping in icy jewelry. He went around the passenger's side, opened the front door, and took Kenzie's hand, helping her out.

"Daayuuun! Aye, yo! Hoomiez, cuz! That's ol' girl from Wild 'n Out!" someone yelled as the red head's shiny, white, Jimmy Choo pumps touched the ground.

"Aye, Justinaa! Yo, spit some bars for a nigga, yo!" another shouted.

"Damn, she thick as hell now!" one more yelled.

Kenzie, looking as delicious as a hot sweet potato pie loaded with brown sugar and cinnamon in a little white top that looked like a leather band wrapped around her breasts and upper back, a tiny blue leather micro mini-skirt, hair done up, and a little makeup and jewelry on with sweet smelling perfume, couldn't do anything but laugh at how people really though she was Justina Valentine.

Then, Kenzie heard someone else shout, "What the fuck you bring a white bitch to the hood for, nigga?!" It was a female yelling.

"Yeah! Can't find a Black woman?"

The rude remarks instantly made Kenzie angry. They made her remember the insults tossed at her all through her life just because she looked white. Xavier saw her looking around, trying to get a lead on who said it, likely so she could go get them.

"Aye, Ma," he called to her, taking her hand into his. She turned her head and looked at him with a frown.

"Now I know you ain't worried bout them salty ass hoes talkin' shit while they stuck outside, and we walk right in."

"No," Kenzie capped, pouting, still trying to see who said that stuff out the side of her right peripheral. "Fuck them hoes."

"Right. Fuck 'em. Let's go inside and cut loose," Xavier told her, then as the bouncers stepped aside, one opening the door, Xavier and Kenzie entered, no pat down, feeling the bass of Wiz Khalifa's *Tweak is Heavy* pounding.

Inside Club Hood, blue lights flickered and flashed. There was shiny blue paint on the walls, mirror ceilings, and glassy concrete floors. It was wide open with a long bar off to the far side and high tables with bar stools set across from it while a spacious dance floor was in the rear. So many people were in the club partying, having a ball, and it was only Thursday.

Xavier led his lady through the crowds of people. Majority were rocking blue, as Homewood was Crip City, still standing strong, while so many others wanted to be Blood.

Who Am I? by Wiz came on just then. Xavier took her to the bar, and they ordered drinks. He ordered her a Long Island Iced Tea and Remy Martin for himself. Kenzie sipped the sweet liquid fire and grimaced.

"Woo! Damn, that is freaking strong!"

Xavier laughed after sipping his.

"That shit gon' have you on ya ass by the last drop, bae."

"If we drinkin', how we getting home? Uber?" she asked.

"You already thinkin' about leavin'?" He sipped the drink again.

"No. I was just wonderin', Xavier."

She leaned over to him and licked his face.

"You taste good."

Xavier laughed.

"Yo ass is wild, lil mama."

A pair of hands then suddenly covered his eyes. Kenzie looked and saw a very voluptuous white woman behind her man. She was taller than Kenzie with jet black hair, and her arms were inked up like a tattoo model. She wore a ridiculously tight white bodysuit with a neck strap, open back, and slits in the sides. White pointed toe pumps were on her feet, giving her even more height. Her gold jewelry was adorned with flawless white diamonds, her juicy lips painted glossy red, and her eyebrows tweezed and arched perfectly.

Kenzie swore she was looking at J Woww from the TV show, *Jersey Shore*, and a bit of jealousy burned within her as the girl touched her man.

"Guess whoooo?" the Italian beauty sang, her lips close to Xavier's ear.

He smiled. "Hmmm… with them little big ass hands, I'd say… Miss J Woww."

The girl sucked her teeth and let go, muffing the back of his head.

"Asshole," she called him.

Xavier spun around and stood, empathically giving the girl a brotherly hug. It put Kenzie at ease a little, but she was still curious as to who the chick was.

"What's good, cuz? How you been?" she asked as they released each other.

"All good, Ma. You?" Xavier asked.

"Maintainin', yah mean? Gettin' money, buildin' wealth, still reppin' Steel City Mafia."

She patted the SCM tattoo that was above her right breast, inked into her milky-white skin in blue letters.

Xavier chuckled. "I did it, Ma. Yo, this my lady, Kenzie." He looked at his woman then. "Kenzie, bae, this is Lacey. She been our people since day one. We was all youngins, runnin' around together. She's like a sister to Macho and Tool."

"Nice to meet you, girl," Lacey gave Kenzie a welcoming hug.

"Nice to meet you too, Lacey. That bodysuit is bangin'!" Kenzie told her.

Lacey twirled, showing off her amazingly thick body in the painted-on ensemble.

"That joint you got on is killin' it too, yo! On the homies, you gon' have Zay whoopin' muhfukas in here over you, girl!"

Xavier smiled. "As long as they only lookin'," he replied.

Just then, a big man appeared with his lovely high-yellow completed queen at his side. Perry, in a blue Gucci fit, fresh bald fade haircut, diamond studs in his ears, beard and goatee super crispy, diamond chain around his neck with a diamond Richard Mille on his wrist, and Gucci sneakers on his feet, was looking like the young fresh boss that he was.

His woman was clad in a blue FeFe Couture mini dress with blue five-inch heeled sandals. Her dark brown hair was braided in intricate fishbones, and there were diamond earrings dangling from her ears with shiny flawless stones in the necklace she wore. On her left wrists, a diamond Chanel watch, on her right, a diamond tennis bracelet. Blueberry lipstick graced her perky lips, and black eyeliner lined her lids.

Perry dapped Xavier up like they were brothers, then the woman gave him a sisterly embrace. Xavier introduced Perry's woman to his.

"Baby, this is Felicia, Perry's queen,'" he told her.

Kenzie smiled and hugged it out with the five-foot seven beauty.

"You must be the real deal," Felicia told her, "cause Zay never has had that look in his eyes."

Kenzie grinned an ear to ear smile at that. A glance over at Lacey though showed her that the Italian vixen wasn't all that excited to be in the presence of Perry's lady; and the fact that Felicia didn't acknowledge Lacey, as Perry did, told her that someone had a crush on the six foot five Steel City Mafia goon.

"I hope so," Kenzie replied to Felicia but looked at Xavier. "He's the realest man I have ever met."

"Zay is that dude, yo," Lacey chimed in. "All the ladies want him, but it looks to me like you have him."

"Well," Xavier then said, looking at Kenzie, "wanna dance?"

"Hell muthafuckin' yes! Let's go!" she replied excitedly and all but yanked him toward the dance floor.

***

EVELYN
Evelyn led the way to the new Valdez Transport yard. On the way, she put her new ride through its paces. The power it had was on point. It sailed along the highway like a big yacht doing ninety on a sixty-five mile an hour stretch. The air ride suspension, along with her air ride seat, made the ride feel so bump less, like rolling on clouds.

Arriving, she turned in, followed by her Caribbean goon escort, Prince, and her girls, who had a tail behind each of them. Evelyn went toward where her 780 Volvo was and parked her much bigger 880 next to it. She was about to get out when she got a call from Nena.

"What up?"

"Aye, is everything okay?" Nena asked, sounding worried.

Evelyn's eyebrows furrowed.

"Why you ask that?"

"Because me, Gloria, Tool, and Gold Mouth's guys was finna meet Javi, Michelle, Macho, Yessy, and G-Baby at the Skillet, but when we all got there, cops was deep as fuck, then Tool dipped off in a rush, leaving me and Gloria with the Jamaicans."

Evelyn hadn't heard a single thing. It pissed her off to be left out.

"I'ma call my brother. Where y'all at now?"

"Turning into the yard," Nena told her.

Evelyn looked and saw Nena's sparkling new 389 car-hauler entering the yard. Right behind her was Gloria in her used but rebuilt 2013 International 9900i Eagle with four black SUVs behind.

Shit! Prince! Evelyn panicked, looking at where her BMW was parked with him inside.

"I'll let you know, Nena!" Evelyn hurried up to say, then she ended the call, jumped out of her truck, and ran to her BMW, hopping in behind the wheel right as Gloria rolled in her direction.

Evelyn put it in drive and floored it. Prince flew back into his seat. She swerved around Gloria's truck and left behind tire smoke as she sped out of the lot.

"Um… everything aight?" Prince asked as she yanked the wheel to the right and whipped it out of the yard onto Kilbourne Lane, shooting south toward Russell Road.

"Yup, mhmm. Just, um, I gotta pee real bad," Evelyn capped, "and I don't feel like bein' around nobody else but you, Papi."

"Well, make a nigga feel all good 'n shit, why don'tcha?" He chuckled as she came to Russell and hit a hard left.

"Oh, I plan to as soon as we make it to the Ramada in Waukegan. We done playin' games, boo. We finna go get our grown folk on and lay up for the rest of the night," she declared with every intention on going crazy on him at the hotel room she had already reserved for them.

***

"Okay then. Now, I know where y'all be at. Bet," he said, seeing the silver Beemer his cousin had unknowingly led him to as he followed Prince and the big convoy of trucks and SUVs to the Dominican's yard.

He pulled off, heading in the opposite direction, already trying to put a plan together on how he could make his move on the rich ass truck drivers and get rich as hell off of their coke and their money.

***

VICTOR
Nancy, face down, her ass up, let Victor finish off by stuffing himself into her asshole. She let him do him. The powerful pain meds she was on had her not caring about anything but climaxing.

"Oh sh-sh-shhhiiit!" he cursed as his nut came with such force that it nearly crippled him.

He pulled out of her ass and exploded, cumming all inside of her crack. Nancy purred at the feeling of his semen splattering in her crevice, coating her bootyhole. She started laughing then, the prescription pain pills and the alcohol she'd sipped making her feel so goofy.

"¡Ay, Victor," Nancy moaned as she laid down on her stomach. "You make me feel so good, mi amor."

Victor got off the bed, grinning at her.

"Victor is more than my name, mamacita. I'm a winner through and through."

His iPhone beeped just then. Naked, dick swinging, Victor walked toward his long dresser across the way from his enormous, luxury, California king-sized bed to where his phone set. On the screen, he saw he had a video call, but he didn't recognize the number.

Picking the phone up, Victor decided to answer it. The screen came alive, and he saw the face of the woman who had beaten his ass at the gas station: ChaCha Sandoval.

"Adivina quién, mal parido," she said to him with a sly smirk.

"H-H-How the fuck did you get this number, puta!" Victor demanded to know.

ChaCha laughed. "Come on, papo chulo. You know who I am and what I can do. You are so far behind, pendejo."

Victor grinded his teeth.

"What the hell do you want, bitch?"

"I would like for you to watch that 'bitch' word, but bitches love callin' other people bitches." ChaCha laughed again, making Victor even angrier.

"But check it out, yo. Someone wants to meet you officially."

He waited as ChaCha handed the phone to another person. When Victor saw the face of Javier Valdez, he seethed in fury.

"¡Pinche puto! You want war with me! I'm the motherfucking king of the Midwest!"

Javi burst out laughing at him.

"You sound like a goofy, my man. Don't nobody give a fuck about all that other shit. Right now, it's about yo punk bitch ass and me. Bring ya ass to the bar on Route 173 and Green Bay Road in Zion now, mamahuevo."

Victor's eyebrow rose.

"Why the fuck would I do that, stupid ass?"

"Because I said so, bitch! Yo grandmother's life depends on it."

Victor's heart nearly stopped when the screen went to his grandma, tied up in a chair, gagged, and blindfolded. A big group of people surrounded her, which included four dogs.

"You got one hour to be there," Javi continued. "If you even think about runnin', number one you's a real live bitch for leavin' yo g-ma hangin'; two, we'll find you. You have no idea who we have planted in ya circle. Try me, bitch."

The screen went black, then suddenly, the phone's screen cracked.

"What the fuck?" Victor said in shock.

"¿Papi? ¿Que pasa?" asked Nancy, still lying on the bed, head on the pillows, body glistening with sweat.

"I gotta get outta here!" he said more to himself, panicking.

He was not going to give his life for his grandmother's.

Fuck that old hag! She's only got a few years left anyways! I'm going to Mexico! he thought to himself as he hurried into his big walk-in closet, grabbing a duffel bag and going to his hidden safe.

He put his eye to the retina scanner, and the door unlocked. Inside were stacks of cash, all hundreds, gold bricks, diamond jewelry, and rare rubies. He quickly filled his duffel with over three million in cash alone and nearly double in jewelry and precious stones.

Victor then hurried to get dressed in jeans, a shirt, and sneakers. From a gun rack next to his safe, he grabbed two Glock 22s, both with thirty-round clips, tucked them in his bag, then after grabbing a VR60 semi-auto 12-gauge shotgun with four five-round magazines, sliding one into the AR-15 looking shotty, he left up out of the closet, ready to hit it.

Nancy had already put her dress back on. Her right foot had a flat on it, while her left foot's cast prevented any shoe from fitting on. She had her big crocodile skin Chanel tote bag's strap over her shoulder and a worried look on her face.

"Come on! Let's go!" Victor urged, rushing toward his bedroom doorway with the stuffed bag and shotgun.

"But... but... where are we going, Victor?" she asked, hobbling along behind him.

"Mexico! You're coming with me, baby!" he told her, leading the way out to get to the built in four car garage.

Nancy followed him out of the beautiful mansion into the fancy garage where two exotic cars and two SUVs set. Victor opened the rear hatch door to his new Mercedes G550 truck and put the bag in. Nancy stood by the door, watching. Victor came and hit the garage door opener button. The port in front of the G-Wagen began rolling up.

Victor suddenly heard footsteps. He turned and saw a very tall man with long dreadlocks wearing a black hoodie, jeans, Tims, and no mask. He carried a Glock 18 in his hand, and the look in his eyes said he was not there for a friendly visit. Victor immediately upped his shotgun and pointed it at the man.

"One more step, motherfucker! Come on!"

Click clack!

Victor then felt the barrel of a gun touch the back of his head.

"Drop it, pendejo," he then heard.

His heart dropping, Victor recognized Nancy's voice instantly. The man walked right up to him, towering over him. Victor lowered his gun and felt the heavy weight of defeat on his shoulders.

"What will your father think of this, Nancy? You whoring yourself to me to help these fuckers?" Victor asked.

She laughed. "My father died a looong time ago," she said, now with no accent whatsoever. "The person you believed was him was just a damn farmer. I am the head honcho. And my name is Guera, puto."

Guera then struck him in the back of his head with her Sig Sauer 9mm, dropping him to the floor with a gaping wound in his head gushing blood. Dazed, seeing double, Victor looked up. He saw Guera standing next to the tall dread head. The man patted her on the ass.

"Good job, Ma. We'll be sure to make good on our side of the deal," said Tool, "and I'm very sorry about my crazy ass brother's traffic plan."

Guera smiled. "Estoy bien, Papi. I've been trying hard to find reliable transport for my yayo for months now, dude! Believe me! The pain is worth it!"

"You good now, Ma. Me and my lil bro got you," Tool promised her, then he looked down at Victor. "¿Oye, mamahuevo?"

He tucked his automatic handgun in his waistline then grabbed Victor, snatching him up off of the ground like he weighed nothing. Victor looked up into the eyes of a demon and felt more fear than he'd ever felt before. He was so scared that he was close to shitting on himself. Tool grinned evilly at him.

"You fucked with the wrong ones, homeboy. I hope you lived a good life," Tool said then head-butted Victor so hard that he knocked him right out.

Chapter 18

EVELYN

Evelyn's back arched up off of the bed as the feeling of sheer bliss overwhelmed her. Her legs were up, wide open, as Prince sucked on her clit like a man addicted to eating pussy. He loved how she tasted, even after a long day of work. He'd been dreaming of getting the sexy Dominican naked since he met her.

"Prince! Oh, God, yes! Shit!" Evelyn cursed, feeling his lips and tongue working her. "Goddamn, baby! Eat this pussy! Just like that!"

Prince groaned as he slurped up her leaking juices, lapping up her honey like a cat drinking milk. Pretty Ricky's *Juicy* enhanced the mood in the room.

In the motel room, the second the door closed, Evelyn was on him. She threw herself at him, and Prince caught all of her. In less than a minute, they were both naked. Evelyn went bananas over his toned tattooed body, but the sight of his long, thick pipe made her pussy thump like a subwater was inside of it.

Feeling her orgasm building, Evelyn's body began trembling. Prince went crazy on her then and made her cum so hard that she went blind for a second.

"Whoa! Holy shit!" she panted, breathing hard to refill her lungs.

"Lemme find out you a rookie, shorty," Prince teased as he lifted his face from between her thick thighs.

"Rookie?" Evelyn sat up then, surprising him by muscling him onto his back. "I got yo rookie, boo-boo," she replied, wrapping a hand around his pipe. "Lay back, relax, and enjoy, baby."

Prince inhaled a deep breath as Evelyn positioned herself on all fours alongside him. She held his cock up and lowered her head down, starting off by planting a kiss on the bulbous tip, followed by swirling her tongue around it. She ran her tongue down the shaft to his balls then sucked them into her mouth.

"Oh sshhsshhiiiiit! Goddamn!" Prince cursed, as Evelyn pleasured his nut sack and used one hand to jerk his dick.

It'd been a few years since Evelyn had been intimate with a man, but she hadn't forgotten, and she planned on going hard on Prince. From his balls, she went lower and licked the spot between his nuts and asshole. Prince nearly jumped out of his skin but didn't stop her. She made her way back up to his dick, and opening her mouth wide, she engulfed him, taking him to the back of her throat, going balls deep. She slowly released then repeated a few more times. Hearing him moaning, groaning, cursing, feeling his dick spasm in her mouth, aroused Evelyn even more. It gave her great pleasure to know that she was pleasing Prince.

She started sucking him faster, using a hand to stroke him at the same time. Prince cursed so much that a sailor would be appalled. She had him feeling so good that he was already close to busting his nut. But he didn't want to bust yet. He wanted to feel that wet-wet right now! Prince snatched his dick out of her mouth, flipping her over onto her back. He pushed her legs out wide and putting the tip of his ten-inch rod at her swollen opening, he gently entered her.

"Ssss mmmm ssshiiit, Prince! It's so thick and big!" Evelyn moaned, feeling him fill her up.

"All for you, baby. This dick is all for you," he told her, starting his stroke game. "Is this pussy mine? Can I have it?"

"Yeess! Yeess, Prince! It's yours! Get it all! ¡*Metemelo*, Papi! Fuck me deep!"

"Oooo, yeah, speak that shit to me while I go deep up in this pussy," Prince requested, taking her hands and pinning them down on the bed as she wrapped her legs around him.

Evelyn started talking super dirty to him in Spanish then.

"¡Metemelo mas duro, Prince! ¡Aayy, dios mio, me encata!" she cried out loudly as Prince started going faster, giving her long, deep strokes. "¡Damelo el platano, Papi! Damelo todo! ¡Hazme venir duro!"

It all made Prince go harder on her. In minutes, after power fucking her, Evelyn climaxed hard again, blasting Prince, cumming all over his dick. He went to flip her into another position, but Evelyn again took over just as Lil Durk's *My Beyonce* featuring Dej Loaf came on. She pushed him onto his back, jumped on top of him, and slid down on his pole.

"Fuck! Damn, this pussy feel so muthafuckin' good!" Prince groaned, gripping her thighs as Evelyn started riding him.

He sat up to suck a breast, but she pushed him back down.

"This my show, motherfucker! I run this shit!" she declared, looking like a sexy devil to him right then.

Evelyn leaned forward, her hands on his chest, gripping his muscular pecs. She rode him like she was in love with him. He filled her cave up so good, hitting a spot that hadn't been touched in years. She grinded on him, leaned down farther, and kissed his lips, never once losing her rhythm. She felt herself ready to release again as the song ended, and Lil Wayne's *On Fire* came on. Seconds after, Evelyn came for the third time.

Prince then got her on all fours and slid up inside her from the back. He started hitting it hard. The way her phat, juicy, sweaty ass jiggled every time he went in excited him even more. The pussy was so hot and tight that he felt like she was made just for him, and he intended on keeping it like that.

He stroked long and hard, pounding her, pulling her hair, smacking her ass, talking so dirty to her that his words alone could make her nut. Prince roared as he felt his nut threatening to explode. He started fucking her as hard as he could, putting his lower back into it. Evelyn screamed out in bliss.

"Oohhh, Prince! Yeeesss! Oohh, yeeesss, Papi!"

She came again just then. Right before Prince could come, Evelyn jumped forward, snatching him out of her, then got him onto his back again. She took his cumming dick back into her mouth again and sucked him wildly until Prince filled her mouth with cum. She sucked and jerked until he was empty. Then, she spit all of it back out onto his dick and slurped it all back up. Prince was gone.

"Goooooddamn! Yo ass bout the freakiest, baddest chick I dun' ever had, shorty!" he exclaimed, exhausted from Evelyn's crazy sex game.

She giggled after swallowing his semen.

"You ain't seen shit yet, playboy, but best believe… you will. I need to go though. Gots to get back to the yard and handle some biz."

"Fa sho. You mine now. You know that, right?" Prince asked her.

Evelyn smiled. "You better do me right. I'm not nice when someone does me wrong, and I have a really protective family."

Prince nodded his head. "I know how Latinos be, Eve. Y'all asses ride together and will die together."

"Naw, boo-boo. We don't die," Evelyn countered, sitting upright on the bed. "The ops do though. So don't become one," she warned, knowing that Prince had no clue of the extent her warning carried.

***

The two walked hand and hand out of the hotel into the dimly lit parking lot toward Evelyn's BMW. She really wished she didn't have to leave, but she just knew Gloria was blowing her phone up, and she'd dipped off before her Jamaican goon detail could get with her. Evelyn let go of Prince's hand for a minute to get her iPhone out and turn off 'Do Not Disturb' mode. Seconds after, missed calls and notifications from Goldmouth, Jamaica, ChaCha, Nena, Javi, Michelle, Diego, Maritza, Macho, Tool, Yessy, G-Baby, Danny, and of course Gloria came back to back with numerous texts demanding she answer the phone.

"Oh, shit… I think I'm in trouble," Evelyn said.

"Trouble? With who?" Prince asked.

Boc! Boc! Boc! Boc! Boc! Boc! Boc! Boc! Boc! Boc!

The sudden gunfire made Evelyn instinctively drop to the ground and scoot in between two cars. Glass and shrapnel flew as bullets hit the cars she'd ducked between. The shots stopped after a few more blasts. Then, Evelyn heard the sound of an engine gun, followed by screeching tires. Then silence.

"Prince?" she called out, not seeing him. "Prince? Papi?"

Evelyn saw him then, laid out on the ground from under the car to her right.

"Prince!" she screamed and jumped up, running to him.

Blood stains grew on his chest and abdomen. He struggled to speak. His eyes were wide open with terror as the agonizing pain of the hot slugs in his body crippled him.

"Shit! Oh, God! Prince!" Evelyn immediately took off her shirt and pushed down on his gunshot wounds, trying to stop the bleeding. "Heelp! Somebody help me please!"

A few people were looking out of the windows. Members of the hotel staff came running out and saw the outcome of the gunshots they'd all heard.

"Help is on the way, ma'am!" a custodian told her, coming to help press a towel on Prince's wounds.

Suddenly, a car screeched to a stop right next to them, making a few people jump back out of fear of more shooting. Evelyn looked and was almost blinded by the blue lights, but looking at the car, she recognized it as the big body Audi that Prince hopped out of earlier that evening. When she saw the face of the man her brother had beat the hell out of at a Burger King and tossed over a counter, while her big cousin trashed his mans, that was said to have been killed by Evelyn's future sister-in-law's bullets, Evelyn almost peed her pants.

***

STACKS
Standing there, looking down at his cousin and the golden-haired beauty, Stacks wanted to pull out his Glock and put one in her dome for what her family did to his homie, Rambo, and how they nearly killed him too. He was so glad that he knew how to swim. Seeing his cousin bleeding on the pavement, dying before his eyes, Stacks reached down to scoop Prince up.

"Wh-What are you doing?!" Evelyn demanded as she rose up, covered in Prince's blood.

Stacks grilled her with a venomous glare.

"My cousin is not gonna die because of the slow ass paramedics," he told her then hurried to get Prince on the backseat of the Audi. "I'm here, fam," he said to his big cuz, who was barely holding on. "I got you."

"I'm coming with him!" Evelyn declared, non-negotiable.

Stacks snarled at her.

"Get in the back with him and hold the bleeding in with that towel on the floor. If my cousin dies, shorty, then you die."

Ignoring the threat, Evelyn jumped in the back seat and grabbed the towel. She hurried to press it over the bleeding gunshot wound while Stacks jumped behind the wheel. He slammed it into drive, mashed the gas, and tore up out of the hotel's lot and raced south on Green Bay Road toward Washington Avenue. The emergency room was just minutes away from where they were, but Prince was losing so much blood that she was already fearing the worst. Stacks heard her begging and pleading for his cousin to hold on.

"Hold on, baby! We're almost there! Just a few minutes, Prince! Keep your eyes open! Please!"

Stacks' own eyes filled with tears, but he quickly wiped them away before they could fall.

"Prince! No! Don't close your eyes!" he heard Evelyn then plead right as he got to the light at Green Bay Road and Washington. "Prince! No! Open your eyes! Priiiiince! Noooo! Oh, my Gooood!"

***

KENZIE

Kenzie purred her feeling of satisfaction as Xavier busted his nut between her ass cheeks. In a private dance room, they couldn't help but to rip each other's clothes off and go at it all over the place – on the couch, on the bar, on the small stage at the front of the room, by the stripper pole, and on the carpeted floor where they currently laid. Xavier pulled himself out of her asshole and blasted her crack with hot globs of cum.

"Mmmm, baby, you got me feeling so good," she told him as he stood up, panting hard, sweating his ass off.

"A woman like you deserves it hot and wild every time she wants it," he told her.

He took her by the hand, helped her up, then fixed her thong and pulled her pantyhose back up for her. Kenzie yanked him to her afterwards and kissed him long and hard, heating herself up all over again.

"Save some of that fire for later, Ma," Xavier chuckled. "We got all night."

"I'm just an Energizer Bunny, bae. I keep goin' 'n goin' 'n goin', With the right man, I'm unstoppable."

Xavier laughed his ass off.

"Remember you said that," he told her, ready to meet that challenge just as his phone started ringing.

He grabbed it off of the bar and saw it was ChaCha calling.

"¿Qué lo qué, prima?" he asked her then put it on speaker while he grabbed his clothes to get dressed.

"We got him, yo," ChaCha said.

Kenzie heard ChaCha speak. She saw confusion register on Xavier's face.

"Got who?" Xavier asked with furrowed brows.

"Bitch-tor Gomez. Guera did her job perfectly, though she got a little banged up in the process. Antonio is… crazy, but Tool hand delivered that punk ass bitch to us personally."

"¡Diablos! Guera though?" asked a bewildered Xavier. "I thought she was dead!"

"Sometimes people have to let others think they won in order for other people to actually win, papito. ¿Me entiendes?"

"I dig. Well, I can shoot back and come help out. I'm already knowin' that Guera gon' be in need of our services."

"True. Soon, Xavier. Stay with Kenzie and Neveah and the ol' heads. When it's time to help her out, we'll all roll together."

Xavier sighed. "Alright, cool. Aye, where's my brother and my sis at? They with you now?"

"Javi is, but nobody knows where Evie is. She dipped off when she and some of her girls brought their new trucks in. Someone was drivin her whip; nobody could see who. And her little ass left without Goldmouth and his crew. Gloria is pissed, yo."

"Maan, what the fuck goin' on out there, cuzzo?" Xavier asked, as Kenzie came and wrapped her arms around him.

"Shit's been crazy, yo. Real shit, but no te apure, papacito. It's all about to end and go back to normal."

"Okay, ChaCha. Yo, tell Gloria to call me."

"Shiiit, her ass dun' went M.I.A. too. But she'll turn up. Word on my motha though, yo. It's all good. But, um, when you get back, there's a new member of the Valdez Transport team."

"Uh… okay? You said that like a new hire is a big deal."

ChaCha chuckled. "When you get there, tu vas a ver, papa! Love you, lil dude."

"Love you too, prima."

The call ended. Kenzie kissed him on his cheek and asked if everything was okay.

"Accordin' to ChaCha, it will be," he told her, though he just could not fight the feeling that the drama wasn't even close to being over.

***

JAVI

"I been waitin' for this, mamahuevo!" growled Javi as he squaded up.

Victor Gomez got on his guns as well. He had no choice. In a big, windowless room, he was surrounded by nearly twenty members of the Valdez family, which included Macho, Tool, Yessy and G-Baby; ChaCha, Jamaica, Juanito, Carolina, and along with them was Michelle, Kiara, Jada, Nena, O-Boy, Bull, Cadillac, JB, EZ Money, Pete, and Thurgood. Michelle held Demon's and Diamond's leashes wrapped around her wrists, holding the angry Sicilian mastiffs. Their eyes were locked onto Victor. They saw food.

Macho held his pit bull's leash, and Yessy held her rottweiler's. They wanted to let the dogs eat so badly, but

Javi wanted the honor of tearing Victor up himself. He wanted to box.

"¡Vamos, mamahuevo!" Javi demanded. "Fuck yo ho ass waitin' for?! You want to live then fight!"

Javi gave Victor his word that if he kicked the fair one with him, they would not kill him nor his grandmother. Victor had no choice but to believe it. He refused to beg for his life like a coward. If Javi wanted a fight, Victor was going to give him one.

Michelle held the leashes to her dogs as tight as she could, though she wanted to let them go to rip Victor apart and be done with it. She stood by, preparing to watch her man be a man and handle business. Victor, shorter than Javi by a few inches, had a slight disadvantage, but his will to live, mixed with his skilled boxing background, fueled him to not back down. He ran up on Javi, swinging calculatedly. Javi ducked the first, side-stepped the second, but the third caught him on the chin. The blow was powerful enough to daze him.

"Aye! Boy, you better not let him hit'chu again, yo!" Yessy shouted as she held the leash of her angry rottweiler, who was practically about to pull her arms out of their sockets. "All the work we did to get him here! Lose and I'ma beat chu myself!"

"Get his ass, Javi!" shouted G-Baby then.

Michelle stayed silent but was cheering her man on inside of her head. *You got this, baby! Come on! Be that tigueraso I know you are! ¡Agarra 'se mamahuevo!*

Demon and Diamond were going ballistic, barking madly, dying to be let go to jump in with Javi and tear the threat to pieces. Macho, his red nose, and his brother were silent, watching intently as everyone else was.

Bink! Bink! Crack! Wham!

Victor rocked Javi four times in a row, sending him to the floor on his ass.

"Javier! ¡Levántate ahora mismo y pelea!" demanded Juanito, growing furious watching his great nephew losing.

"¡Levantáte!" Carolina then shouted at him.

"Yeah, puto!" Victor spat on the floor by Javi, glaring at him with a wicked smile. "Get the fuck up so I can knock your bitch ass back down in front of your family!"

Javi looked over at his fiancée, their eyes meeting. He saw her pleading with him to get up and handle it, then she silently mouth *get up* to him. Grinding his teeth in anger, Javi's fury suddenly spiked. He ignored the stinging pain in his chest. Woth fire in his eyes, Javi looked at Victor.

Victor grinned at him. "Yeah, good job, puto. Now let's dance!"

Victor rushed him again, locked onto Javi. He swung a hard right, but faster than the blink of an eye, Javi disappeared from his line of sight.

Crack!

"Aagggh!" Victor shouted in pain as a blow to the tip of his jaw from the left snapped his head to the right.

Then, he yelled, "¡Puta madre!" He was angry that he had just gotten his bell rang.

He jumped around and saw Javi at his left. He rushed at him again, swinging four times when he got close enough to him. Not a single one of them connected. Javi countered with a move he'd learned from his big cuz, Macho.

Michelle watched her future husband maneuver a downward right spin, of which he came back up with his left elbow. Victor didn't even see it coming until Javi's elbow crashed into the center of his face so hard that it shattered his nose. Victor howled in agony as he hit the ground, gushing blood. Javi grabbed him by his shirt and snatched him up. He went in on Victor then, beating the rest of his face in until he was a bloody pulp.

"Yes! Yes! Get him! ¡Matalo ese putp mamahuevo, Papi!" Michelle shouted excitedly.

Javi's crew whooped and hollered, cheering their boss on. The ladies cheered for him, egging him on. Juanito had taken out his iPhone and was showing his younger brother, Diego, and his sister-in-law, Martiza, via video call how their grandson was beating the fuck out of Victor Gomez.

"Bitch, talk that shit now!" Javi seethed.

Crack! Crack! Crack!

"Come on! I can't hear you!"

Javi continuously beat Victor until he was unconscious. He dropped the rival enemy to the floor and glared down at him. Off to his side, he heard Demon and Diamond barking furiously. He looked over at ChaCha and nodded his head. She nodded her head, then going to the door, she opened it up and yelled, 'Bring 'em in!' to someone.

Michelle smirked evilly as two dread heads led in Valencia Gomez, followed by two more leading Alejandro Gomez, Victor's father. Javi slapped the shit out of Victor until the bloody and swollen man came to. Javi grabbed him and held him so that he could see his g-ma and his pops.

"¡Ay, dios mio! ¡Mi nieto!" his grandmother cried, overly distraught to see her battered grandson.

Alejandra was furious. He looked at his longtime nemesis, Juanito, sneering.

"You will pay for this, pendejo!" the old Mexican hissed through clenched teeth.

Juanito stayed stone faced, not at all worried, but Carolina didn't. She walked right up to the much taller man and…

Crack!

She rocked his jaw so hard that a few of his teeth broke.

"¡Callate la maldita boca!" she snapped. "¡Por lo que tu hiastes, te vas a morir! ¡Tu y tu fucking madre, mamahuevo!"

"¡Vete al infierno!" Alejandra shot back.

"You first, bitch," chimed in ChaCha, catching his attention.

Alejandra looked over just in time to see the Amazon tall beauty winding up as if she was getting ready to hit a homerun with a Louisville Slugger, but instead of it being a bat… she had a machete.

"*Noo!*" he screamed in panic, eyes wide as dinner plates.

"Die!" ChaCha yelled, and as the two Jamaicans held Alejandro where he stood, she swung the machete as hard as she could.

The blade sliced right through Alejandro's face, chopping from his eyes and up clean off. The Jamaicans let the dead kingpin fall to the ground. Blood immediately began pooling around his corpse.

"Noooo! Alenjandroooo!" screamed Valencia.

Smack!

Carolina smacked the old woman across her face.

"¡Callate, puta!" she yelled.

Then, ChaCha swung the machete on Victor's grandmother, slicing her head off at the neck. Victor's heart dropped as he watched his father and g-ma die before his eyes. Javi continued to make him watch as Yessy let her rottweiler go get Salina's head. Maliante snapped his powerful jaws onto the severed head and carried it over to Victor as if to taunt him. Victor saw his grandma's dead eyes staring right at him. Suddenly, his bowels loosened up, and he shit on himself. Javi released him then kicked Victor in the back of the head.

"Puto sucio mamahuevo," he cursed as the foul odor began filling the room.

"Okay! Okay! I surrender!" Victor cried out. "Let me go and I'll disappear! I swear! You'll never see my face again!"

Javi chuckled. "I know. Don't 'een trip, homeboy. We gon' help you out with that."

He grabbed Victor again and started dragging him toward the door.

"Wait! Wait! I'll pay you!" Victor yelled as he left a blood trail on the ground. "I've got millions! Pleeaase!"

The family followed as Javi dragged the pleading man toward a much bigger area. Inside was a big industrial meat grinder that had gotten rid of many enemies before Victor Gomez. Javi let Victor go and went to turn on the pulverizer.

Victor heard it turn on, saw it, and tried to crawl away. He was snatched up from the ground by Tool before he made it a foot away from where he was.

"Fuck you think you goin', bitch?" the massive Dominican dread head said and lifted Victor up over his head.

"Nooo, nooo, noooo! Waaaaaiit!" Victor pleaded as he saw the spiked meat crushing rollers in the entry chute.

"Wait these nuts, mamahuevo!" Tool replied then tossed Victor in face first.

Everyone watched as the man was sucked into the pulverizer. As his body inched in, bloody bits of meat and bone was spewed out from the other side, piling up into a plastic bin. In less than a minute, Victor Gomez was reduced to shredded meat. Javi shut the machine off then. All was silent. Michelle let the dogs' leashes go. Macho and Yessy let their dogs go too. All four dogs ran to the bin of raw meat and dug in, snapping up bloody chunks like crocodiles stuck in a feeding frenzy.

Michelle went to her fiancé and hugged him tightly. Javi hugged his future wife back even tighter. He kissed the top of her head then looked at his family and friends. Then, suddenly, Macho started singing.

"Na na na naaa… na na na naaa! Heey, heey, heey, gooodbyyyeee, biiitch!"

Everyone burst out laughing at him.

"¡Este hombre esta loco!" Yessy laughed as she went and wrapped her arm around her man.

Chapter 19

JAVI

Two Weeks Later…

Tears rolled down Michelle's face. The news had her completely devastated. More than distraught, she was heated, but more than that… she was hurt. Javi felt broken. His future wife bawled her eyes out when it was confirmed. Angela was pregnant, and she swore it was Javi's child. Michelle tried to kill her with her bare hands, but ChaCha and Yessy stopped her. Pregnant women were off-limits, even if they deserved to get their wig split by an ax.

Sitting in a bedroom, wrists and ankles tied up on a bed in one of ChaCha's hide-out houses in Fox Lake, Illinois, Angela smiled smugly as she listened to Javi's fiancée crying her eyes out from outside the closed door. She continued listening to Javi plead with her to forgive him. Then, Angela heard a loud *slap* followed by a, "Fuck you, Javi!'

Angela burst out laughing. The door flew open just then, and Michelle ran in again, swinging on Angela so hard that the Boricua flew sideways off the bed, hitting the floor with a thud.

"Laugh again, bitch! I dare you!" she screamed, stomping toward her.

"Michelle! Enough, Mama!" ChaCha came and grabbed her before the skilled killer could find something to use as a weapon.

Angela laid on the floor, feeling like her head was ringing bells. The door slammed shut again then and locked.

***

"Javier! Just go! Give her some damn space!" ChaCha demanded, glaring at him so venomously.

Michelle bawled in ChaCha's arms, heart hurting so bad. She couldn't even look at him.

"I love you, Michelle," Javi wept. "I'm so sorry, baby. I swear."

"Javi, Papa, please just take a few days somewhere," ChaCha told him. "This is hard on her."

Javi nodded, then he left them alone, heading outside to his Monte Carlo SS. He started up the engine and put it in drive. Pulling out of the driveway, he made his way toward Beach Park to get home and pack some clothes and shoes. On the way, he called the one person he knew wasn't pissed at him for getting another woman pregnant.

"Can I stay at y'all crib for a few days, cuz?" Javi asked.

"Uh… do you feel that it'd be safe for you to do that?" Macho countered.

"Why wouldn't it be? What you finna swing on me when I show up?"

Macho laughed. "Who? Me? Naw. You can come through, lil cutty. Just… oh… never mind. See you when you get here, yo."

Javi ended the call then tried his sister for the millionth time as had everyone else.

Straight to voicemail,

"Where the fuck are you, Eve? Dammit, man!" he cursed, worried sick that something had happened to her.

***

EVELYN

Evelyn laid on the ER's ICU bed next to the comatose Prince. The heart monitor beeped, an oxygen machine was breathing for him, and an IV was in his arm. He had so many bloodstained bandages that it looked like he was popped up by a chopper.

The TV in the room was on. The TV show, *Ice Road Truckers,* filled the fifty-five-inch screen. *Ice Road Trucker* queen, Lisa Kelly, was tearing down an icy, muddy hill in a white Kenworth W900L with a flatbed trailer on. The daring female trucker was having a ball, riding the shit out of her truck. Normally, the show always put Evelyn in a good mood, but Prince being so close to death just wouldn't let her cheer up at all.

The door to the room opened up just then. She looked up and saw Stacks enter with a big bag of Wendy's. Evelyn stayed quiet as he walked up to her. He took out a crispy chicken sandwich, fries, and a cookie, handing it to her. Evelyn thanked him and grabbed the chicken sandwich, starving. It'd been nearly three days since she'd eaten anything.

Stacks watched her nearly eat her food in less than fifteen seconds. He shook her head at her.

"Yo people kill me homie," he told her, "and came real close to takin me out too."

"You wouldn't leave me alone, man! My brother and cousin are extremely protective of me!"

He chuckled. "I have a feelin' that my cousin was shot because of you, shorty."

Evelyn swallowed hard.

"I heard about yo family. Y'all got that 'caine by the truckload," Stacks said.

"I don't know nothin' you talkin' about, dude."

"Bitch!" Stacks jumped up and rushed her, grabbing her by the throat.

Evelyn clawed at his hands, trying to loosen his grip, but he was strong.

"Lie to me again and I swear next time you gon' be bleedin' out of twelve bullet holes!"

He loosened up then, allowing her to suck air back into her lungs. Evelyn was heated, but she knew she could not beat him. He was not small, and his dark eyes filled her with fear.

"This what you gon' do, jo. On the five, yo ass finna bring me some of them bricks yo people be bringin' in. I need a hunnid!"

"I... I can't! My family wouldn't allow it!" Evelyn cried.

"Then don't tell 'em! All I know is yo ass better do what the fuck I'm telling you, or I will catch you slippin'! I know where yo brother's truckin' company is. Get yo people shot up if you want. Nobody will see me comin!" he told her. "Just like you didn't!" he added.

Evelyn normally would laugh at such a thing, but when it came to the safety of her loved ones, she couldn't bring herself to play with their lives.

"Okay! I'll do it! I'll get you coke, man!"

Stacks grinned then. He dug in his pocket, pulled out a new prepaid phone, and gave it to her.

"I know y'all bring it once a month. Someone I know has y'all schedule. I better hear from you a couple days before, shorty, or on Ghost, you gon' have a lot of blood on yo hands."

Stacks exited the room without another word, leaving Evelyn with tears of fear pouring down her face.

***

XAVIER

"Hooooneeey! I'm hooome!" shouted Xavier playfully as he made a wide turn into the Valdez Transport yard in his Icon W9, pulling his unloaded RGN lowboy.

Laid out on the bed with her daughter and Precious, Kenzie laughed at him.

"Goofball," she called him.

Xavier saw three quarters of the VT trucks were gone as usual. His crew was out along with Evelyn's crew with the exception of Evelyn's two Volvos and Nena's new 389 Peterbilt. Most of Javi's crew was out except for Sergio's, Pistol's, and Black's Kenworths and Javi's Pride and Class.

Parked at the office was a new silver Lincoln Navigator sitting next to a red Mercedes S550 and a turquoise Nissan 350Z. Xavier wondered if they belonged to new hires. He didn't recognize either of them.

Xavier backed his truck up next to a spare RGN lowboy trailer. Kenzie helped him unload all their bads, then Xavier took them to his Range Rover, putting them in the back. While Kenzie let Precious out to stretch as she and Neveah did too, Xavier went inside the office to see if anything was there for his heavy haul division.

The second he walked back toward the main office area, he ran into a familiar looking woman, an extremely gorgeous chick wearing a tight yellow-gold bodycon dress with gold pumps and black Prada glasses. She had long, sexy, black hair in a bun and wore red lipstick. Xavier's eyes went wide when he recognized her in two seconds.

"Vanessa!" he exclaimed in shock.

She smiled at him flirtatiously.

"Hey, Zay. Long time no see."

"Ahem!"

A throat being cleared from behind made Xavier turn only to see the worst possible sight ever.

Pamela stood next to Nena… and they looked pissed!

"Welcome back," said Nena very sarcastically.

Pamela's eyes were blood red with anger. Then, to make matters even worse, another girl walked up just then.

Oh, shit… What the fuck?! Xavier thought to himself as he locked eyes with a furious Keisha.

"You know yo ass is grass, right?" she asked as the three of them started advancing toward him.

Xavier stepped backwards, past a very confused Vanessa, until his back was against the wall. He had nowhere to run now.

***

JAVI

Crack!

Yessy's fist crashed into Javi's jaw the second he stepped into her and Macho's big, luxurious house over in Zion. Macho grimaced as his cousin hit the hardwood floor.

"Daaaayuuum, cuz... See? I asked if you thought it was safe to come here, yo," Macho said, reaching down to help Javi up while Yessy stood there seething, ready to hit him again.

Their dogs sat a few feet away, watching it all.

"You could've said yo girl was gonna ring my bell, cuz," Javi replied, rubbing his jaw.

"You're lucky that's all I did! Fucking cheatin' ass!" Yessy snapped, taking a step toward him.

"Bae, chill." Macho stopped her and held her back. "I think he gets it. Go finish your set and I'll be right there."

Yessy walked off, her workout clothes drenched in sweat as was Macho, who looked huge in his sweat-soaked tank top, Nike shorts, and Nike trainers.

"You couldn't warn me, cuz?" Javi asked as Macho shut and locked the door.

"Nope. Yessy threatened great bodily harm upon me if I did," Macho told him, "and she don't make idle threats."

They went into the kitchen, dogs following. The big chef's kitchen with marble floors, granite countertops, and stainless-steel appliances was grand and sparkling. At a breakfast bar, Javi sat on a bar stool while Macho got him a cold Presidente from the Sub-Zero.

"Relax, lil cutty. Michelle gon' be aight. Give her a little time and maybe take an ass whoopin' but you'll be back in ya own bed soon."

Javi sighed and popped the top of his beer. He took a big gulp then looked at his cousin.

"What am I gon' do, cuz? That bitch is really pregnant!"

Macho shrugged. "Maybe not cheat on ya lady anymore? With thots?" he suggested.

Javi looked at him.

"Like you ain't fuckin' G-Baby!"

"Burr!" Macho shouted, Gucci-Manning him. "Yo ass tweakin' with that. That's me and my lady's best friend, fool!"

"Uh huh. Tell ya story walkin', cuzzo," Javi replied and took another gulp of the Dominican beer.

***

VANESSA

"Hey! Hey! Stooop!" Vanessa yelled as Kenzie swung windmill punches at Pamela and Keisha.

Kenzie saw nothing but red when she walked in and saw the three women ganging up on her man. She ran up on Nena but ended up rocking Pamela, laying her out. Keisha, knowing exactly who Kenzie was, got on her guns and started throwing those hands. She was much shorter than Kenzie, so she took more hits than she landed.

"Yoo! Chill out!" Xavier yelled, not even knowing what to do.

Kenzie kept on going at it with Keisha, hyping her up, sticking and moving like a seasoned boxer. Xavier wanted to get his woman and dip out of there, but just then, Neveah walked in on the whole scene with Precious and freaked out when she saw her mother fighting. Her scream temporarily distracted Kenzie enough for Nena, who had fallen back into the background, to run up and swing. She punched Kenzie hard in her jaw, ringing her bell. Keisha then delivered a hard blow to Kenzie's side. A loud fart escaped her, then Kenzie's bowels evacuated as she hit the floor.

"Mommy!" Neveah screamed, terrified.

Xavier ran up on Keisha and Nena, livid. He grabbed them both by their throats and snapped.

"Get the fuck out now!"

He smacked their heads together, then letting them go, Keisha and Nena took off. Xavier snatched up Pamela, smacked her awake, and pushed her out as well. Vanessa was wowed by Xavier regulating like a G. She was so turned on, always had been whenever he let the beast in him come out. She looked at the red head. A very large brown stain was at the seat of her pink leggings with a bulge. Vanessa smelled the foul odor and wrinkled her nose.

"Kenzie!" Xavier picked her up off of the floor. "Bae, are you okay?"

"No! Take me home! Please!" Kenzie cried, embarrassed to high hell.

Neveah stood, crying, by Precious. Precious whimpered and whined, feeling Kenzie's anguish. Xavier took Kenzie's hand, grabbed Neveah, then hurried them out with Precious following them. Vanessa, still standing there, was just stuck. *God, he looked so goood... I have to get him back! He is mine!* she proclaimed to herself, already plotting out a way back into his heart.

***

JAVI

Javi woke up in the middle of the night from hunger pains. He regretted not eating the dinner Yessy cooked, BBQ chicken, sweet corn, and mashed potatoes, and for dessert, she had red velvet cake with vanilla frosting and sprinkles. There were plenty of leftovers, so Javi got up and left out of the spacious guest room to go down to the kitchen.

***

Maliante and Dreams laid out by his feet as he ate a few chicken wings and corn. He ate a slice of cake then looked at his phone. There were no texts back from Michelle, but he did get a reply from Evelyn. He'd asked what the hell was up with her. She replied, "Nothing. Needed a break from everyone. I'm safe. Love you."

Javi texted her back that he loved her too then sent an, "I love you," to Michelle.

Sighing, Javi felt the need for some air. He went up to the guest room, put on a tank top, socks, and sneakers with his Nike basketball shorts, then grabbing his keys, he headed back down, disarming the alarm using the code Macho gave him.

Javi hopped up into his SS, which was parked next to Macho's big, white Bentley Flying Spur along with Yessy's super rare BMW M7 Pininfarina Gran Lusso Coupe concept, one of very few in the world that Macho dropped just short of a million on to gift to his woman. He started the engine. A text from Macho came in.

Where is you going, cuz? It's 3 a.m.

Javi responded.

For a drive. Can't sleep.

Macho's response came fast.

Naw, yo. Bring yo ass back in! Nothin good is out there right now!

Javi texted back.

Chill, cuz. I'll be back soon. Just need to clear my head.

He put his phone in the cup holder then backed out of the two-vehicle wide driveway and rode up to exit the subdivision where Macho had just over eighty big luxurious homes after dropping tens of millions for the one hundred acres of bare residential land and having it built up into his own neighborhood. He then gave it all to his woman.

He hopped on Green Bay Road and headed south. The two-way road was nearly deserted, save for a passing car every so often. Lost in deep thought, Javi couldn't stop kicking himself for going astray. The flesh was weak, but his mind had always been strong. He had the best woman that a man could ask for, a ride or die chick by definition. She was his heart. She was the air that he needed in order to breathe. Without her, Javi felt like he was suffocating.

I have to go see her. I need my woman, he thought to himself as the sound of the powerful LS7 under the hood of his Chevy hummed.

Cruising at the speed limit, Javi was stuck on auto pilot while his mind was stuck on his pregnant fiancée. He was lost without her, her heart bleeding. He knew he had really fucked up, but he just couldn't allow it to be when he knew how fed-up women thought after discovering their boyfriends, baby daddies, or husbands had dove up into another woman's pool. Javi was unable to fall back.

Not even realizing how far from his cousin's house he already was, Javi's mind came back, and he saw he was passing Kenosha Road. Doing the speed limit, southbound on Green Bay Road, Javi reached out to the touchscreen head unit to turn on the music. Gucci Mane's *She Like Me* featuring Yo Gotti started playing seconds later. The six twelve-inch L7 Kickers in the Monte Carlo's trunk came alive and started pounding when the beat dropped.

Closing in on the Beach Park area, Javi started practicing what he was going to say to his woman when he got to their mansion. A quarter mile ahead, Javi could see the traffic light at the intersection for Green Bay Road and Wadsworth Road. He took a deep breath and exhaled, feeling like a piece of shit for what he did to Michelle. He was so stuck in his thoughts that he was oblivious to the vehicle that was tailgating him until, suddenly, red and blue lights started flashing. Javi blinked his eyes and saw the cop car behind him. His eyebrows furrowed. He looked at the digital dash and saw he was doing the speed limit, and his music wasn't even that loud.

"Fuck this pig want, man?" he wondered as he began slowing down to pull over right before he got to where 33rd Street was.

He came to a stop on the shoulder and put it in park. Turning down his music, Javi waited, both hands on the wheel. The bright spotlight on the cop car turned on and nearly blinded him as the officer aimed it at the rear of his SS. He held his hand up to deflect some of it.

Before Javi even realized the cop had gotten out of the car, he heard a tap on the passenger's side of his car. He looked to the right and could only see the officer's dark colored, polo style shirt. Javi hit the button on his door and rolled the passenger window down. The cop then leaned down, revealing his face. The second Javi saw the man's mug, he went wide eyed.

"How are you, Mr. Valdez?" asked Detective Barrera, smiling a shit eating grin. "Out for a late-night cruise?"

Stuck, Javi could do nothing but stare at the man.

"Hey, I'm sorry I haven't gotten back to you about your… uh… stolen," the detective said sarcastically, "truck and trailer. I've been at a few funerals that I had to plan and attend."

"Oh… okay… sorry for your loss," Javi finally said.

"I'm sure you are," Detective Barerra again said in a sarcastic way.

Javi started feeling a chilly vibe coming from the cop. It made him contemplate pulling off on his ass and taking the man on a high-speed chase.

"Uh… is there a reason you pullin' me over?"

"Oh, yeah! That! Well, you see, I was actually just out for a drive, and I see this nice ass Super Sport roll past me. I love the color blue, and the racing stripes are cool. Then, you got it rolling on some really nice wheels, man! What are these? Twenties?"

"Add four inches," Javi told him, looking at Barrera with a puzzled expression.

"Wow! Man, this car is beautiful! And it sounds like there's a monster under the hood! It can't be the original engine."

"Detective? I have things to do, sir. Did I do something wrong?"

"You mean besides trafficking large quantities of cocaine for your family? Or all the murders you've committed in just the past few months?"

"No, I mean like was I speedin'? Or my music too loud?"

The detective burst out laughing. Javi looked at the old Mexican and shook his head.

"No, Mr. Valdez. You weren't speeding nor was your music too loud."

"Then why are…"

"Hey… sir! What are you doing?" the detective asked, cutting Javi off.

Javi's eyebrow rose up.

"I'm sittin here. Duh."

Barrera's eyes bugged wide just then.

"Hey! Hey! Don't do it! Sir! Stooop!" he yelled, taking a step back, putting his hand on his holstered Glock 27.

"Yo, what the fuck is you on, dude?" Javi asked, getting weirded out.

"Sir! Get your hands off of the gun! Hands off now!" Barrera shouted, then he drew his weapon and pointed at Javi's face.

"Oh, shit," Javi gasped in shock as he looked into the barrel of the .40 cal.

Then…

Boc! Boc! Boc! Boc!

To Be Continued…

Lock Down Publications and Ca$h Presents
Assisted Publishing Packages

Due to an increase in the price of services we have increased our prices. The prices below reflect the price increase as of 11/1/24.

BASIC PACKAGE	UPGRADED PACKAGE
$699	$1000
Editing	Typing
Cover Design	Editing
Formatting	Cover Design
	Formatting
	Upload eBooks to Amazon
	Upload Paperback to Amazon
ADVANCE PACKAGE	**LDP SUPREME PACKAGE**
$1,400	$1,700
Typing	Typing
Editing (line editing/content)	Editing (line editing/content)
Cover Design	Cover Design
Formatting	Formatting
Copyright Registration	Copyright Registration
Proofreading	Proofreading
Upload eBooks to Amazon	Set up Amazon Account
Upload Paperback to Amazon	Upload eBooks to Amazon
	Upload Paperback to Amazon
	Advertise on LDP's Amazon and Facebook Page

***

Other services available upon request.
Additional charges may apply

Lock Down Publications
P.O. Box 944
Stockbridge, GA 30281-9998
Phone: 470 303-9761
Email: lockdownpublications@gmail.com

Submission Guideline

Submit the first three chapters of your completed manuscript to ldpsubmissions@gmail.com. In the subject line add **Your Book's Title**. The manuscript must be in a Word Doc file and sent as an attachment. Document should be in Times New Roman, double spaced, and in size 12 font. Also, provide your synopsis and full contact information. If sending multiple submissions, they must each be in a separate email.

Have a story but no way to send it electronically? You can still submit to LDP/Ca$h Presents. Send in the first three chapters, written or typed, of your completed manuscript to:

LDP: Submissions Dept
P.O. Box 944
Stockbridge, GA 30281-9998

DO NOT send original manuscript. Must be a duplicate. Provide your synopsis and a cover letter containing your full contact information.

Thanks for considering LDP and Ca$h Presents.

NEW RELEASES

BLOODLINE OF A SAVAGE 1-3
THESE VICIOUS STREETS 1-3
RELENTLESS GOON 1-3
BY PRINCE A. TAUHID

THE BUTTERFLY MAFIA 1-3
BY FUMIYA PAYNE

A THUG'S STREET PRINCESS 1&2
BY MEESHA

CITY OF SMOKE 3
BY MOLOTTI

GET IT IN SLUGS 1 &2
BY B. STALL

STANDING ON HER BUSINESS 1&2
BY DG SANTANA

STEPPERS 1,2&3
THE REAL BADDIES OF CHI-RAQ
BY KING RIO

THE LANE 1&2
BY KEN-KEN SPENCE

THUG OF SPADES 1&2
LOVE IN THE TRENCHES 2
CORNER BOYS
BY COREY ROBINSON

TIL DEATH 3
BY ARYANNA

TIPPIN' THE SCALES 3 | DIESEL

THE BIRTH OF A GANGSTER 4
BY DELMONT PLAYER

PRODUCT OF THE STREETS 1-3
BY DEMOND "MONEY" ANDERSON

NO TIME FOR ERROR
BY KEESE

MONEY HUNGRY DEMONS 1-2
BY TRANAY ADAMS

HUB CITY MENACE 1-3
BY J. WHITE

A THUGGISH PASSION 1&2
LAND OF DA HOOLIGANZ 1-4
KILLAZ ON STANDBY 1&2
BY IRA B.

FO'EVA ROLLIN 1&2
BY ASSA RAYMOND BAKER

THE LEVEL UP 1&3
BY LUXURY KING

Coming Soon from Lock Down Publications/Ca$h Presents

IF YOU CROSS ME ONCE 6
ANGEL V
By Anthony Fields

A THUGS STREET PRINCESS 3
By Meesha

CORNER BOYS 2
By Corey Robinson

THA TAKEOVER
By Keith Chandler

BETRAYAL OF A G 2
By Ray Vinci

SAVAGE FAMILY EMPIRE 1&2
SOULLESS GOON 1,2&3
THE DIRTY SIDE OF MONEY 1,2&3
By Prince

FOR MY ENEMY'S SAKE
AMBITIONS OF A SLIDER
FRESH OFF DA PORCH
By IRA B.

THE TRUCKLOAD 1-4
TIPPIN' THE SCALES 1-3
BAD BITCHES WIT GUNZ 3
PROBLEM SOLVED 2
By Christopher "Diesel" Hornezes

Available Now

RESTRAINING ORDER 1 & 2
By **CA$H & Coffee**

LOVE KNOWS NO BOUNDARIES 1-3
By **Coffee**

RAISED AS A GOON I, II, III & IV
BRED BY THE SLUMS I, II, III
BLAST FOR ME I & II
ROTTEN TO THE CORE I II III
A BRONX TALE I, II, III
DUFFLE BAG CARTEL I II III IV V VI
HEARTLESS GOON I II III IV V
A SAVAGE DOPEBOY I II
DRUG LORDS I II III
CUTTHROAT MAFIA I II
KING OF THE TRENCHES
By **Ghost**

LAY IT DOWN I & II
LAST OF A DYING BREED I II
BLOOD STAINS OF A SHOTTA I & II III
By **Jamaica**

LOYAL TO THE GAME I II III
LIFE OF SIN I, II III
By **TJ & Jelissa**

IF LOVING HIM IS WRONG…I & II
LOVE ME EVEN WHEN IT HURTS I II III
By **Jelissa**

PUSH IT TO THE LIMIT
By **Bre' Hayes**

BLOODY COMMAS I & II
SKI MASK CARTEL I, II & III
KING OF NEW YORK I II, III IV V
RISE TO POWER I II III
COKE KINGS I II III IV V
BORN HEARTLESS I II III IV
KING OF THE TRAP I II
By **T.J. Edwards**

WHEN THE STREETS CLAP BACK I & II III
THE HEART OF A SAVAGE I II III IV
MONEY MAFIA I II
LOYAL TO THE SOIL I II III
By **Jibril Williams**

A DISTINGUISHED THUG STOLE MY HEART I II & III
LOVE SHOULDN'T HURT I II III IV
RENEGADE BOYS 1-4
PAID IN KARMA 1-3
SAVAGE STORMS 1-3
AN UNFORESEEN LOVE 1-3
BABY, I'M WINTERTIME COLD 1-3
A THUG'S STREET PRINCESS 1&2
By **Meesha**

A GANGSTER'S CODE 1-3
A GANGSTER'S SYN 1-3
THE SAVAGE LIFE 1-3
CHAINED TO THE STREETS 1-3
BLOOD ON THE MONEY 1-3
A GANGSTA'S PAIN 1-3
BEAUTIFUL LIES AND UGLY TRUTHS
CHURCH IN THESE STREETS
By **J-Blunt**

CUM FOR ME 1-8
An LDP Erotica Collaboration

TIPPIN' THE SCALES 3 | DIESEL

BLOOD OF A BOSS 1-5
SHADOWS OF THE GAME
TRAP BASTARD
By **Askari**

THE STREETS BLEED MURDER 1-3
THE HEART OF A GANGSTA 1-3
By **Jerry Jackson**

WHEN A GOOD GIRL GOES BAD
By **Adrienne**

THE COST OF LOYALTY 1-3
By **Kweli**

BRIDE OF A HUSTLA 1-3
THE FETTI GIRLS 1-3
CORRUPTED BY A GANGSTA 1-4
BLINDED BY HIS LOVE
THE PRICE YOU PAY FOR LOVE 1-3
DOPE GIRL MAGIC 1-3
By **Destiny Skai**

A KINGPIN'S AMBITION
A KINGPIN'S AMBITION II
I MURDER FOR THE DOUGH
By **Ambitious**

TRUE SAVAGE 1-7
DOPE BOY MAGIC 1-3
MIDNIGHT CARTEL 1-3
CITY OF KINGZ 1&2
NIGHTMARE ON SILENT AVE
THE PLUG OF LIL MEXICO 1&2
CLASSIC CITY
By **Chris Green**

TIPPIN' THE SCALES 3 | DIESEL

A GANGSTER'S REVENGE 1-4
THE BOSS MAN'S DAUGHTERS 1-5
A SAVAGE LOVE 1&2
BAE BELONGS TO ME 1&2
A HUSTLER'S DECEIT 1-3
WHAT BAD BITCHES DO 1-3
SOUL OF A MONSTER 1-3
KILL ZONE
A DOPE BOY'S QUEEN 1-3
TIL DEATH 1-3
IMMA DIE BOUT MINE 1-6
DYING FOR LIKES
By **Aryanna**

A DOPEBOY'S PRAYER
By **Eddie "Wolf" Lee**

THE KING CARTEL 1-3
By **Frank Gresham**

THESE NIGGAS AIN'T LOYAL 1-3
By **Nikki Tee**

GANGSTA SHYT 1-3
By **CATO**

THE ULTIMATE BETRAYAL
By **Phoenix**

BOSS'N UP 1-3
By **Royal Nicole**

I LOVE YOU TO DEATH
By **Destiny J**

I RIDE FOR MY HITTA
I STILL RIDE FOR MY HITTA
By **Misty Holt**

LOVE & CHASIN' PAPER
By **Qay Crockett**

TO DIE IN VAIN
SINS OF A HUSTLA
By **ASAD**

BROOKLYN HUSTLAZ
By **Boogsy Morina**

BROOKLYN ON LOCK 1 & 2
By **Sonovia**

GANGSTA CITY
By **Teddy Duke**

A DRUG KING AND HIS DIAMOND 1-3
A DOPEMAN'S RICHES
HER MAN, MINE'S TOO 1&2
CASH MONEY HO'S
THE WIFEY I USED TO BE 1&2
PRETTY GIRLS DO NASTY THINGS
By **Nicole Goosby**

LIPSTICK KILLAH 1-3
CRIME OF PASSION 1-3
FRIEND OR FOE 1-3
By **Mimi**

TRAPHOUSE KING 1-3
KINGPIN KILLAZ 1-3
STREET KINGS 1&2
PAID IN BLOOD 1&2
CARTEL KILLAZ 1-3
DOPE GODS 1&2
By **Hood Rich**

THE STREETS ARE CALLING
By **Duquie Wilson**

STEADY MOBBN' 1-3
THE STREETS STAINED MY SOUL 1-3
By **Marcellus Allen**

WHO SHOT YA 1-3
SON OF A DOPE FIEND 1-4
HEAVEN GOT A GHETTO 1&2
SKI MASK MONEY 1&2
By **Renta**

GORILLAZ IN THE BAY 1-4
TEARS OF A GANGSTA 1/&2
3X KRAZY 1&2
STRAIGHT BEAST MODE 1&2
By **DE'KARI**

TRIGGADALE 1-3
MURDA WAS THE CASE 1-3
By **Elijah R. Freeman**

SLAUGHTER GANG 1-3
RUTHLESS HEART 1-3
By **Willie Slaughter**

GOD BLESS THE TRAPPERS 1-3
THESE SCANDALOUS STREETS 1-3
FEAR MY GANGSTA 1-5
THESE STREETS DON'T LOVE NOBODY 1-2
BURY ME A G 1-5
A GANGSTA'S EMPIRE 1-4
THE DOPEMAN'S BODYGAURD 1&2
THE REALEST KILLAZ 1-3
THE LAST OF THE OGS 1-3
By **Tranay Adams**

MARRIED TO A BOSS 1-3
By **Destiny Skai & Chris Green**

KINGZ OF THE GAME 1-7
CRIME BOSS 1-4
By **Playa Ray**

FUK SHYT
By **Blakk Diamond**

DON'T F#CK WITH MY HEART 1&2
By **Linnea**

ADDICTED TO THE DRAMA 1-3
IN THE ARM OF HIS BOSS
By **Jamila**

LOYALTY AIN'T PROMISED 1&2
By **Keith Williams**

YAYO 1-4
A SHOOTER'S AMBITION 1&2
BRED IN THE GAME
By **S. Allen**

TRAP GOD 1-3
RICH $AVAGE 1-3
MONEY IN THE GRAVE 1-3
CARTEL MONEY 1&2
By **Martell Troublesome Bolden**

FOREVER GANGSTA 1&2
GLOCKS ON SATIN SHEETS 1&2
By **Adrian Dulan**

TOE TAGZ 1-4
LEVELS TO THIS SHYT 1&2
IT'S JUST ME AND YOU
By **Ah'Million**

TIPPIN' THE SCALES 3 | DIESEL

KINGPIN DREAMS 1-3
RAN OFF ON DA PLUG
By **Paper Boi Rari**

THE STREETS MADE ME 1-3
By **Larry D. Wright**

CONFESSIONS OF A GANGSTA 1-4
CONFESSIONS OF A JACKBOY 1-3
CONFESSIONS OF A HITMAN
CONFESSIONS OF A DOPE BOY
By **Nicholas Lock**

I'M NOTHING WITHOUT HIS LOVE
SINS OF A THUG
TO THE THUG I LOVED BEFORE
A GANGSTA SAVED XMAS
IN A HUSTLER I TRUST
By **Monet Dragun**

QUIET MONEY 1-3
THUG LIFE 1-3
EXTENDED CLIP 1&2
A GANGSTA'S PARADISE
By **Trai'Quan**

CAUGHT UP IN THE LIFE 1-3
THE STREETS NEVER LET GO 1-3
By **Robert Baptiste**

NEW TO THE GAME 1-3
MONEY, MURDER & MEMORIES 1-3
By **Malik D. Rice**

CREAM 2-3
THE STREETS WILL TALK
By **Yolanda Moore**

THE STREETS WILL NEVER CLOSE 1-3
By **K'ajji**

LIFE OF A SAVAGE 1-4
A GANGSTA'S QUR'AN 1-4
MURDA SEASON 1-3
GANGLAND CARTEL 1-3
CHI'RAQ GANGSTAS 1-4
KILLERS ON ELM STREET 1-3
JACK BOYZ N DA BRONX 1-3
A DOPEBOY'S DREAM 1-3
JACK BOYS VS DOPE BOYS 1-3
COKE GIRLZ
COKE BOYS
SOSA GANG 1&2
BRONX SAVAGES
BODYMORE KINGPINS
BLOOD OF A GOON
By **Romell Tukes**

CONCRETE KILLA 1-3
VICIOUS LOYALTY 1-3
BLOODY MONEY BAGS
By **Kingpen**

THE ULTIMATE SACRIFICE 1-6
KHADIFI
IF YOU CROSS ME ONCE 1-3
ANGEL 1-4
IN THE BLINK OF AN EYE
By **Anthony Fields**

THE LIFE OF A HOOD STAR
By **Ca$h & Rashia Wilson**

NIGHTMARES OF A HUSTLA 1-3
BLOOD AND GAMES 1&2
By **King Dream**

GHOST MOB
By **Stilloan Robinson**

HARD AND RUTHLESS 1&2
MOB TOWN 251
THE BILLIONAIRE BENTLEYS 1-3
REAL G'S MOVE IN SILENCE
By **Von Diesel**

MOB TIES 1-7
SOUL OF A HUSTLER, HEART OF A KILLER 1-3
GORILLAZ IN THE TRENCHES
OOPS CRY TOO 1&2
THE DAUGHTER OF A CARTEL BOSS
By **SayNoMore**

BODYMORE MURDERLAND 1-3
THE BIRTH OF A GANGSTER 1-4
By **Delmont Player**

FOR THE LOVE OF A BOSS 1&2
By **C. D. Blue**

KILLA KOUNTY 1-5
TENDER
By **Khufu**

MOBBED UP 1-4
THE BRICK MAN 1-5
THE COCAINE PRINCESS 1-10
STEPPERS 1-3
SUPER GREMLIN 1-4
A GANGSTA'S SON
By **King Rio**

MONEY GAME 1&2
By **Smoove Dolla**

A GANGSTA'S KARMA 1-5
By **FLAME**

KING OF THE TRENCHES 1-3
By **GHOST & TRANAY ADAMS**

BAD BITCHES WIT GUNZ 1&2
PROBLEM SOLVED
By **"Christopher Diesel" Hornezes**

QUEEN OF THE ZOO 1&2
By **Black Migo**

GRIMEY WAYS 1-3
BETRAYAL OF A G
By **Ray Vinci**

XMAS WITH AN ATL SHOOTER
By **Ca$h & Destiny Skai**

KING KILLA 1&2
By **Vincent "Vitto" Holloway**

BETRAYAL OF A THUG 1&2
By **Fre$h**

COUNTDOWN OF A KILLA 1&2
SEX, MURDER AND GOD 1&2
GUNS DOWN, BOTTOMS UP 1&2
By Lo-Life

THE MURDER QUEENS 1-7
By **Michael Gallon**

FOR THE LOVE OF BLOOD 1-4
By **Jamel Mitchell**

TIPPIN' THE SCALES 3 | DIESEL

HOOD CONSIGLIERE 1&2
NO TIME FOR ERROR
By **Keese**

PROTÉGÉ OF A LEGEND 1,2&3
LOVE IN THE TRENCHES 1&2
By **Corey Robinson**

THE PLUG'S RUTHLESS DAUGHTER 1&2
By **Tony Daniels**

BORN IN THE GRAVE 1-3
CRIME PAYS
By **Self Made Tay**

MOAN IN MY MOUTH
By **XTASY**

TORN BETWEEN A GANGSTER AND A GENTLEMAN
By **J-BLUNT & Miss Kim**

LOYALTY IS EVERYTHING 1-3
CITY OF SMOKE 1-3
By **Molotti**

HERE TODAY GONE TOMORROW 1&2
By **Fly Rock**

WOMEN LIE MEN LIE 1-4
FIFTY SHADES OF SNOW 1-3
STACK BEFORE YOU SPLURGE
GIRLS FALL LIKE DOMINOES
NAÏVE TO THE STREETS
By **ROY MILLIGAN**

PILLOW PRINCESS
By **S. Hawkins**

TIPPIN' THE SCALES 3 | DIESEL

THE BUTTERFLY MAFIA 1-3
SALUTE MY SAVAGERY 1&2
By **Fumiya Payne**

THE LANE 1&2
By Ken-Ken Spence

THE PUSSY TRAP 1-5
By **Nene Capri**

DIRTY DNA
By **Blaque**

SANCTIFIED AND HORNY
by **XTASY**

BOOKS BY LDP'S CEO, CA$H

TRUST IN NO MAN
TRUST IN NO MAN 2
TRUST IN NO MAN 3
BONDED BY BLOOD
SHORTY GOT A THUG
THUGS CRY
THUGS CRY 2
THUGS CRY 3
TRUST NO BITCH
TRUST NO BITCH 2
TRUST NO BITCH 3
TIL MY CASKET DROPS
RESTRAINING ORDER
RESTRAINING ORDER 2
IN LOVE WITH A CONVICT
LIFE OF A HOOD STAR
XMAS WITH AN ATL SHOOTER

www.ingramcontent.com/pod-product-compliance
Lightning Source LLC
Chambersburg PA
CBHW071154260626
47162CB00003B/1050